Finding Eliza

Stephanie Pitcher Fishman

Rebecca Hills
Books

Finding Eliza by Stephanie Pitcher Fishman
Published by Rebecca Hills Books
Edited by Staci Troilo (www.stacitroilo.com)
ISBN-13: 978-0692238097 (Rebecca Hills Books)
ISBN-10: 0692238093

Visit the author at www.stephaniefishman.com.

Thank you for taking the time to read this work. Please consider leaving a review on the page that you purchased this book. By reviewing it and telling your friends about it, you will help me share my word with the world. I greatly appreciate your support.

FOR ERICA & CAITLIN
Never stop dreaming.

Let all bitterness and wrath and anger and clamor and slander be put away from you, along with all malice. Be kind to one another, tenderhearted, forgiving one another, as God in Christ forgave you.

Ephesians 4:31-32 (NIV)

CHAPTER ONE

Fall held deep meaning for Lizzie. It meant that the pain of summer was over. The transition into a busy schedule after the lazy days of summer usually brought a renewed joy and purpose into Lizzie's life. Not this year. This year it marked the second decade since she became an orphan. The brightly colored leaves of fall couldn't wipe the stains of death away with the same ease of years past. This year, it lingered.

Twenty years ago she had been a happy twelve-year-old girl. The biggest tragedy she had faced in life was finding out that Jimmy Thompson was taking another girl to the fall dance.

Did I even go to that dance after all? she thought.

Lizzie tilted her head as if it could allow her to see the past a little clearer. Thinking back, she realized that she couldn't remember one thing about the dance or even Jimmy Thompson.

Shielding her eyes from the mid-day sun, Lizzie took a moment to drink in the colors that rained down around her as the wind sent leaves from above to their resting place in the grass below. Her eyes lingered on the ground as memories flooded back to remind her of how much her father loved the red Georgia clay.

As a child, Lizzie's mother would give a spiritual nature to the clay. She would tell her young daughter, "Lizzie girl, God made us out of clay. He formed us from the muddy earth, and to that earth we will one day return. It's how we're designed."

Growing up, Lizzie sat in church between her parents every Sunday. She knew from years of Southern Baptist sermons that her life here wasn't meant to be permanent. Still, the idea that it would end terrified her. It was as stifling as the summer's heat, pulling the air out of her body and bringing on panic as if she was fighting for her own life right there and then. Heaven was for those who were old and unattached to her. It wasn't a place she wanted to go any time soon.

Fear always appeared on Lizzie's face first. It crept across her eyebrows as the muscles in her forehead squeezed her fair skin into heavy crinkles and crevices. With a sly grin and a quick wink, her father would lighten the mood by reminding her that the Hines family wasn't made from just any old dirt.

Elton Hines would take her into his arms and whisper into her ear the most important secret he could pass to his young child. "No need to worry, kiddo. Our clay is strong. God didn't use regular old dirt on the Hines family. We're made from red Georgia clay; God's dirt of champions. Nothing will break it before it's old and brittle. You've got a lifetime to live before that happens."

Her father was wrong. It did break sooner than was necessary.

Stories like these were all she had left of her parents. Sitting on the wooden park bench under her favorite old oak tree, she couldn't help but think about times gone by. She leaned deep into the park bench and squeezed her arms across her body while her father's words and memories flooded her heart. It was almost as if he was whispering in her ear from afar. Lizzie missed her parents with a deep ache that overwhelmed her even two decades later.

A visit to a familiar place like the Everett Springs City Park helped Lizzie shorten the distance between earth and heaven. This small act brought the memories from so many years ago into the present. It was a small, deliberate act of time travel that Lizzie perfected as a child. She could make memories seem like they happened only yesterday. It helped her feel as if her parents were still a part of her day. Adding in a pimento cheese sandwich on toast just like her mother made didn't hurt either. Because of its simple power, she added it to her lunchtime routine whenever the weather would allow.

The park was a beautiful respite from the heat that refused to believe it was already fall. Tucked away among the flowering trees and bushes, the park created an escape in the middle of small town streets and buildings. The jewel in its crown was the garden that surrounded the band stand. The ladies of the First

Baptist Church of Everett Springs prided themselves on the blooms that they could coax out of the red clay each spring. Careful to maintain humility, they dedicated it each year to the members of the church along with a signature verse and flower. Bright colors popped everywhere. In the spring, deep purple irises and bright jewel-toned gladiolas swayed in the breeze while they waited for the zinnias to bring out their color in the fall. Creeping ground cover plants and smaller annuals filled in the empty spaces preventing gaps and holes in the landscape. While she enjoyed the fall foliage, Lizzie missed seeing the Climbing Cherokee Roses that wound around the weathered wooden railings and whitewashed sides of the park's bandstand in the spring. It made her think of her mother.

Deep in her heart Lizzie knew that they weren't the same beautiful plants that Grace Hines pruned during her years of helping with the garden. Still, on days like this they were an acceptable surrogate. To Lizzie, it was good enough to imagine her mother kneeling before them in her ripped and faded jeans. She could almost see her mother wiping the sweat from her forehead with her cotton handkerchief or the back of a scratchy work glove. A delicate smile swept across Lizzie's face as she pictured her mother's hand leaving just a trace of dirt across her brow.

Her father was right: Georgia clay had deep roots into all her memories. Most times it was something that people took for granted. Not Lizzie. She understood the importance that it held. The dust and dirt from her home state's ground intertwined into the entire being of every resident. Even photographs from their childhood showed the stains of the colorful earth. It seeped through cracks in screen doors and open windows on any day with a light breeze. Mothers cursed the sports uniforms baring the raw scars of the minerals that refused to fade no matter how much Clorox they used. Farmers found it caked on machinery while their wives fought to shake it out of their field clothes with great frustration. That dark red dirt was the backdrop of every memory and experience Lizzie had throughout her life. Georgia's red clay was everywhere; it was part of her very soul. She couldn't shake it off if she tried.

Without warning, a familiar Southern drawl snatched her out of her daydream.

"Lizzie! What are you doing all by yourself on a day like this?" a stately older woman called out to her from across the aged stone walk. "It's too pretty an afternoon to be all alone. We need to get you more friends."

Gertrude Hines was a sight to behold in her pillbox hat and her dainty lace gloves that fastened with pearl button at the wrists. Lizzie loved seeing her grandmother's gloved hands. Much like the park, the gloves took her back to her childhood and days of playing dress up in her grandmother's closet.

After her parents' death, Lizzie moved in with Grandma Tru. It was her turn to live in the home that saw her father grow from a boy to a man. The stylish woman before her set aside what should have been her golden days of playing Bridge and lunching with the ladies. Instead, she spent years raising a broken and moody teenager. It wasn't until she was an adult that she realized the sacrifice her grandmother had made to repair her broken foundation. Lizzie knew that her grandmother's actions were a special blessing. She tried to keep that in mind during the times when her intense anger at her situation would take control. Her experience could have been much worse.

"Gran, stop fussing over me. I'm just having myself a think over lunch. I'll head back to the center in a little while. It's so hectic at work lately that I'm happy for some quiet time." Lizzie looked up at her grandmother with a smile. "What are you doing downtown? I thought you had to meet Pastor Aldrich at the church this morning. Isn't it a little late for you to be here?"

"Oh, I was, but of course it got rescheduled. We're looking at the proposed renovations for the old chapel and the Fellowship Hall. You'll have to come see the plans. Everyone is up in arms over the changes. Heaven forbid we change a swatch of carpet or a scratch of old blue paint. They act like it's against the convention rules to have anything but green carpet in a Southern Baptist church." Gertrude waved her gloved hand in the air, dismissing the inferior ideas as if she was swatting flies.

Lizzie couldn't help but giggle at her grandmother.

"I think they are all trying to kill me. It will be death by decorating. I'll end up on some bad cable television special. You just watch."

"Now, Gran, don't be so hard on them. Some of us like the things of the past. I think you are a little partial to them, too. What year did you buy that outfit again?" Lizzie teased as she took another bite of her pimento cheese sandwich.

"Don't you go being cheeky, Miss. No one likes a woman with an attitude. They do, however, like a woman with class and a classic style." True to her humor, Lizzie's grandmother struck a pose on queue. With one hand on her hip and another tilted in the air, she looked just like Coco Chanel on a Paris runway. A slight toss of her head and a raised eyebrow only added to the effect.

"You're absolutely correct, Gran. Your style is definitely beautiful," Lizzie agreed. "However could I have doubted you?"

Gertrude smoothed the bodice of her charcoal gray peplum jacket. How she managed to keep her 1950s style current was beyond Lizzie. Her grandmother could wear a pencil skirt and look fabulous. Gertrude's silver hair stood perfectly coiffed. Her dainty red and black plaid hat set at the perfect angle to finish the ensemble. It was Georgia at the start of football season after all. Everyone had their colors out to support the boys in Athens, even the ladies. Every year Lizzie's dad would take her up to The University of Georgia for the first home game. The Georgia Bulldogs were their favorite, and nothing could compare to being between the hedges at Sanford Stadium for that opening kickoff. Lizzie hadn't been on campus once without her father, and watching it on television just wasn't the same.

"Will you be joining me and the ladies for our meeting tomorrow night?" Gertrude asked.

"I told you that I'd think about it, and I have. I just don't think this is the right week for me to start something new."

Lizzie had been trying to find a way to put her grandmother off yet another time. As much as Gertrude loved genealogy, Lizzie just couldn't find a passion for it. Grandma Tru had been trying since Lizzie was a teenager. Everyone always told Lizzie to live in the present and let go of the past. Getting involved with a hobby based in that nightmare felt counter-intuitive. It was like giving a junkie a fix. Maintaining the present while looking back was difficult and dangerous without the proper preparation. Lizzie was certain that she could say with complete honesty that she was definitely not prepared. Discussing the past now of all times would only remind her of all she had lost the day of her parents' accident. It was fine to remember those days while sitting in a park. Looking back at the past through death certificates and headstones was something else altogether.

"I've just got so much to do at the center. You said it yourself. The kids need me." As a volunteer adviser for the Clarette County Youth Center, she spent her days reaching out to at-risk kids. Labeled at-risk when her parents Elton and Grace died, she had a special bond with the kids there. She could understand what many of them were going through despite the differences in their stories. It was a match made in heaven.

Lizzie threw an angelic grin at her grandmother hoping that the point would land with the appropriate effect. It, unfortunately, did not.

"I've decided that I'm not taking no for an answer this time. You're coming, and that's that," answered Gertrude.

"But Gran…"

"No 'but Gran' this time, young lady. You will accompany me to the church tomorrow for our group. End of discussion. The Gals will love to see you."

Whoever decided that Southern women were sweet and soft spoken hadn't met Lizzie's grandmother. Gertrude could be feisty when she liked. At times the only thing genteel about her was the look of her wardrobe, especially when it involved Lizzie. Gertrude learned to take the bull by the horns when raising that child. Many believed it was the only way they both had survived the adventure.

"You do remember that I'm not a child anymore, right?" Lizzie snapped before finishing the last bite of her sandwich.

Straightening her hat, Gertrude started walking toward the park entrance. "I'm sorry dear. I didn't hear you. My ears are seventy-seven years old, you know." Her grandmother always knew how to play the age card when she needed it to work to her own advantage. "I'll see you tomorrow night. Give my love to Jack." Blowing a kiss into the air, she was off.

Lizzie watched her grandmother cross the road and head toward the church. She couldn't help but say a silent prayer for Pastor Aldrich. She doubted that her

Gran was in the mood to haggle over remodeling ideas any longer. Gertrude left the park armed and loaded for bear. She had accepted the challenge of convincing the board that the chapel was going to be re-decorated to her liking. Brushing the crumbs off her jeans, Lizzie stood to look around the park one last time, saying goodbye to the memories of the past.

CHAPTER TWO

After working all day with the children at the community center, Lizzie was glad to head for home. As she turned onto her long and winding dirt driveway, she felt the weight of the day slide off her shoulders immediately. A happy sigh of relief escaped Lizzie's lips as her home came into view just up the hill.

Not long after they married, Lizzie Hines and Jack Clydell purchased their twenty-five-acre slice of small town heaven. It wasn't filled with modern conveniences like the newer houses recently built in town. The walls held bumps and bruises left behind from a lifetime of memories created by the first owners. Still, the home they nicknamed Clydell Manor represented paradise to the newlyweds.

Hidden away behind the rusted red gate and overgrown flowering bushes, the home sat a half-mile from the road. Lizzie had just enough time to unwind and release the stress of the day as she made the bumpy transition from the road to her front door. Elegant dogwood trees lined both sides of the dirt and gravel drive. Grandma Tru believed that dogwoods brought protection to the families they surround. Whether there was truth to her story or not, Lizzie found peace in the beauty that met her each time she entered or exited the property. She usually preferred to walk among them on stressful days, but she welcomed a drive through the micro-grove all the same. After an emotional afternoon of time travel in the park, the dogwoods' presence brought a smile to her face. Today's memories were good, but they took a toll on her emotions. A slow drive through the trees' deep scarlet and purple fall colors helped Lizzie could transition from past to present before hitting her doorstep.

Polite friends would refer to their home as "lived in" or even rustic. In truth, the Clydell farmhouse was just old. Though it still needed a little bit of work, the white wooden structure was in better shape than when the couple took ownership. Lizzie and Jack loved the feel that the rough wood and asymmetrical boards brought to the home. The large wrap-around porch felt as though it kept the world at bay. The heavy wooden shutters that framed each window further met Lizzie's need for protection.

Over the years, the renovations made were small in comparison to other houses of this age. A screened-in porch added to the rear of the house gave them a place to sit on rainy days while improvements to the barn and outbuildings took care of damage and decay. They didn't long for updated floors or added features. They chose to reinforce the foundation that was already laid by generations past. It didn't matter what others thought about their choices for function over design. Their horses were happier for it, and that was all that mattered to the first-time homeowners.

Their little farm was perfect for their life. Slow, quiet, and filled with warmth, Lizzie needed the grounding that it provided. Jack was all too happy to allow her to put roots down in any manner that pleased her. Luckily the home that pleased Lizzie was a home that pleased him as well.

Lizzie pulled her vintage 1963 Suburban in front of the house. The high polished chrome and navy blue paint showed every speck of dust it picked up from the drive home. She and Jack shared a love of classic cars. He loved the process of restoration; she loved driving down a country road in a machine as heavy and hulking as a mid-century vehicle. Rolling down the manual crank windows brought back memories of warm Sunday afternoon drives when she was a child. She'd trade a sunroof for a vintage automobile any day.

Jack's 1960 Ford F-100 was already parked at the side of the house in its usual spot. The sight of the big, red truck made her smile. She remembered how hard he worked to restore it. Jack's dad had given the body to him when he was in high school. While his friends rallied for a down home rat rod project, Jack would hear nothing of the sort. He built his Ford with blood, sweat, and summer jobs on any farm that would have him because only original parts would do for his baby. Jack would work all day in the fields just to work on the truck by flood light for hours late into the night.

Lizzie had to admit that it was a beautiful piece of machinery, even if it was a Ford.

Sliding off the hot bench seat of the Suburban, Lizzie leaned on the door and stretched her back before walking toward the house. "Hey! Anyone home?" Lizzie called as the screen door bounced back against its frame. She tossed her worn brown leather satchel onto the kitchen table. The pass-through window between the kitchen and the living room let her see that Jack had already helped himself to dinner. He was sitting on the couch in the living room waiting for her, remote in hand.

"Hey, babe. I talked with Miss Tru this afternoon," he said as he chewed another bite of sausage supreme from Luigi's. "She mentioned that she found you in the park having lunch by yourself again. I thought it might be a good night to just sit back and relax with some pizza. Want to be my date?"

Jack was so kind to her. He always knew exactly what she needed. Jack had been a young fifteen-year-old boy when her parents passed away. Even though the two grew up just a few streets apart, Jack didn't pay Lizzie any mind because of their three-year age difference. The summer her family name headlined the town newspapers changed everything. Like other small town country boys, Jack had been driving his dad's truck around their farm for years without worry. Never before did he consider driving to be a threat. Hearing about a car accident that claimed the lives of two adults in the community was a shock to him. Like

Lizzie, he lived his life in complete innocence before the Hines' accident.

Jack came to the funeral with his parents to pay his respects to the lone survivor, a young Lizzie Hines. Seeing how sad and broken she was after greeting mourners at the viewing, he decided to stay behind a while in case she needed a friend. He wasn't sure why at the time, but Jack would later say he felt drawn to the sad girl that he barely knew. That decision would be the start to a romance that was still going strong twenty years later.

Dropping onto the couch, Lizzie tossed off her boots and propped her feet up on the massive wooden coffee table. Snuggling her head against Jack's shoulder, she felt him wrap his strong arms around her. He still worked on his dad's farm on his days off as the County Sheriff's Deputy, and his body showed it. Jack was a handsome man whose personality drew people near just as much as his deep brown eyes did. A quiet night at home with Jack and pizza, her two favorite things, was exactly what Lizzie needed.

"So, tell me. How were the little hoodlums today?" Jack quipped.

"Stop calling them that!" Lizzie smacked him with the first accent pillow she could grab off the couch. She knew he was teasing, but it still got her riled up, which is exactly why he said it.

"My *kids* were great. We spent the morning hanging out in the park with the younger kids until it got too hot. The older kids were focused for once after school. We breezed through their homework and spent the rest of the day just hanging out at the center. It was great to have some downtime to talk. A good time was had by all. I need to spend more time with them like that. I want to find an activity that we can do together that will get them interested in something other than video games. I think that I could build a better connection with them if we had time to just chat outside of something loud or structured."

"You know you do good work with them, right?" Jack turned to look Lizzie in the eyes as he always did when he wanted be sure she would hear him. "You need to think about going back to school. Imagine what you could do with a degree."

"Don't start in on that right now. I'm happy being the one that volunteers and gives back. Don't make it a job or I'll hate it." Lizzie knew he was right, but change wasn't in her nature. "Besides, all I do is show them that someone loves them. I don't need a degree to do that."

Just leave me to what I know, she thought.

Jack was always encouraging Lizzie to go back to college. It wasn't that he thought that she needed more education to be complete. He simply wanted her to have everything that she desired in life. She carried a look in her eyes that showed she longed for more even if she didn't know what 'more' meant.

Lizzie knew that he was just trying to help her fill a void he saw in her life. After her parents' accident, money was tight for Grandma Tru and Lizzie. Her grandmother had plenty of money tucked away for a comfortable life in her retirement. Adding in college costs would destroy that. She couldn't allow Gertrude to make that sacrifice. Lizzie could have taken on student loans but she wasn't one to accept debt if another option existed. She never wanted to leave something behind if there was an accident that prevented her from paying. Jack's position at the Sheriff's Department allowed them to live a debt-free life. They liked it that way. Lizzie wasn't keen on introducing more bills now while life was pleasant.

"So, tell me about you and The Gals," Jack chuckled. Switching off the television, he shoved another slice of pizza into his mouth before turning to face his wife. He couldn't wait to hear the story of how Gertrude Hines had won yet another argument against her granddaughter.

"Gran seems to think that I'll be joining her and the ladies at church on Tuesday."

"Gran is right. I've already made plans to have dinner with the guys that night so you won't be able to use me as an excuse."

Jack knew how Gertrude and Lizzie's relationship worked. Although she could give her grandmother a tough time, everyone knew who held the reins in that family. It wasn't Lizzie.

"Why, Jack Clydell, if I didn't know better I'd think that you had a hand in this." Lizzie laid on her Southern drawl as thick as she could. She added a slow toss of her long chestnut hair for added affect. If she couldn't argue her way out of this with Jack she'd charm him there.

"Don't go all 'Scarlet' on me. You know that I love plotting against you," laughed Jack. "I'm also immune to that hair flick thing so keep on moving, lady."

Lizzie reached for a piece of pizza and settled into the couch. "Gran seems to think that I'll love it, but I just don't think that genealogy is my forte. That's looking at the past. The past is something that we work through, not something that we look for on purpose. I just don't understand why my attendance is so important to her. She's got her friends there. She doesn't need me."

Jack shook his head causing his bangs to land in his eyes just as Lizzie liked them. "You don't understand. Lizzie, you're all she has left. She's the keeper of the family stories. She's the one with the photos and the family names. Miss Gertrude lost her husband and her only son. She's an only child just like you. We haven't had children yet, so guess what girl? You're her only descendant. If you don't care about the family history, no one will. Whether you like it or not, Lizzie, she's going to pass her research to you. It's up to you to decide if you are going to carry on her legacy or let it fade away."

Lizzie knew that Jack was right. Today she thought about a lot of old memories, but she hadn't been thinking of her grandmother in any of them. Her mind had limited her pain by keeping a tight circle of memories in view. When she gave herself permission to think about her family she couldn't ignore the gaping hole that existed in her family tree. The only branches that remained were Lizzie and Gertrude.

Her paternal grandfather, John Hines, had passed away when she was just a little girl. She had seen his photos and heard her grandmother's stories, but she didn't remember him beyond those items. The family stories that Gertrude shared created the only memories that Lizzie had of her grandfather. Family stories and history were important to Gertrude because they proved the ones she loved existed. Less than ten years later, a car crash took the life of Elton, Lizzie's father and Gertrude's only child.

Lizzie found herself thinking back to the night of the accident. In her mind, the sky turned dark and lightening flashed. She could hear the sounds of her mother praying. Before she realized it, she was lost in thought two decades away from the pizza that was growing cold on her plate.

"Lizzie? Honey? Where are you?" asked Jack.

Lizzie looked up to see her husband's concerned face.

"I'm sorry, honey. Did you say something?" Lizzie wasn't sure how long she was lost in thought, but it had been long enough that she didn't hear a word her husband had said.

"I was just saying that I thought it was a good idea for you to go with Miss Gertrude. It will make her happy, and you need something to occupy your thoughts. You seem to have a lot of them lately," said Jack. "It might do you some good to find a little distraction."

Sliding further down into the overstuffed couch, Lizzie wiped her now flush forehead with the back of her hand. The room was warmer than she had remembered. She had lost her appetite as well as her will to fight against both her grandmother and her husband.

"Okay, Jack. I give. I'll go. After all, it's just a little family history." What could go wrong?

CHAPTER THREE

Lizzie's hands gripped the steering wheel as she slowed the Suburban to a stop in front of the church. She hadn't realized how nervous she was until she noticed how white her knuckles had become. The sun was setting, casting a shining light in her eyes that caught her off guard. She rested her head against the wheel to avoid the glare and took in deep breaths to calm her nerves. Breathing out slowly, she regained control and sat up straight in the driver's seat. Before leaving home, Jack had drilled her numerous times to be sure that she would exhibit the proper behavior. Keep smiling. Say she is having fun. Try to enjoy the evening. Check.

"You can do anything for a few hours, Lizzie," he said as she left the house.

Lizzie knew that Jack was right. She could do anything for a few hours. "Time to face 'The Gals'," she said under her breath.

Lizzie swung the vehicle into the closest parking space. As soon as she threw the engine into park she saw some familiar faces. Two ladies in their seventies approached. One rushed to the driver's side door while the other swayed slowly to a stop near the front of the truck. These were Gertrude's trusted friends and confidants. Having been a part of their family long before her father was born, they became the cornerstone of Lizzie's life. Still, she sometimes felt like a victim of the Inquisition when they swarmed her in pairs. Their sweet faces and graying hair hid the truth: they could pry a secret out of a dead man. Lizzie held back a ripple of giggles as she pictured the scene.

Although she knew both of them by name, Lizzie collectively called them "The Gals." From the time Lizzie remembered, the friends called each other "gal" as a term of endearment. Hearing it as a child, Lizzie thought it was their name and began calling them each "gal," much to their amusement. The moniker stuck, and from that point on everyone in their immediate circle called them by the group nickname.

These women had something special. They had experienced joy and pain together for decades creating a bond that acted as both protection and support as needed. When Gertrude lost her husband to a sudden heart attack, The Gals were there. When she lost her son and daughter-in-law in a devastating car crash, The Gals were there. When she wrestled with an emotional and angry teenage girl, again, The Gals were there. As much as Lizzie hated the idea of being part of the genealogy group this evening, she loved how she felt when The Gals were together. It was like Christmas and her birthday all rolled into one because they knew her better than anyone, even Jack. They had become her champions, her cheerleaders, and her best friends. They were her family.

Looking through the window, Lizzie smiled at the faces that greeted her.

"Lizzie, darlin'! I'm so glad you're here!" Lizzie's friend raised her hands in the air and shook them in happy celebration being careful that her purse didn't slide down toward her face. "We've got the family back together again."

"Hey, Ms. Abi! Give me a hug. Have I ever missed you." Lizzie slid out of the truck and into Abi's arms. Her hug was so familiar that Lizzie felt like a young girl all over again. The stress of the day washed away instantly.

Abigail Langdon was one of Gertrude's oldest and dearest friends. They leaned on each other through seven decades of joy and pain. Growing up together in Everett Springs, the two best friends dated and later married local boys who were also best friends. Locals had joked that it was a story made in Hollywood. Like Lizzie's grandmother, Abigail was now a widow. Walter Langdon had passed away following a terrible illness a decade before Gertrude's husband. The ordeal could have left Abigail broken and lonely if it weren't for her strong faith and friendships. Never having any children of their own, Abi and Walt considered Lizzie's father a son of their own heart. After the accident claimed the lives of Elton and Grace, Abigail grieved alongside Gertrude for the loss of her surrogate son. As she had the day Lizzie was born, Abigail once again vowed to be family to the little girl who survived alone. Following through on her promise, she had always been a safe harbor for Lizzie as she navigated her life.

"I see you're jumping on Gran's bandwagon to brainwash me into loving genealogy, too," Lizzie teased.

"You know what, sweetie? I won't have to convince you to like it once you get in there. Before you know it, you'll be chasing dead people like the rest of us! Trust me. It's addictive." Abi couldn't contain her excitement as she waved to the woman who stood just beyond the hood of the Suburban. "Blue - look who's here!"

Agnes "Blue" Meriwether walked around the front of the vehicle and joined the friends. Agnes was another life-long friend to both Gertrude and Abigail. As a child, Agnes loved the color blue so much that everything she wore included it even if it meant adding a thread or an accent of the color. From that point on her nickname became "Blue" to the girls of the town. Like most nicknames, this one was never outgrown. At seventy-eight years young, she continued to be their Blue.

"Please, Abi. We knew it was just a matter of time before our plan got her here," Blue sang in her slow southern drawl. "This'll do you good, baby girl. Just you watch."

"Oh, Blue!" scolded Abigail. "You hush. We promised Tru that we wouldn't say a word."

"Stop acting like I'm letting the cat out of the bag. Lizzie isn't a bump on a log. She knows perfectly well what we're up to with this plot. This child is struggling, and we're throwing her a rope. Now let's get in there before I leave you lunatics and take her out for a drink."

Blue was a good, church-going lady with a fun wild streak and a fondness for a nip of whiskey every now and again. Spunkier than the others, she took immense pleasure in teasing her teetotaler friends. Lizzie adored her way of dealing with life. Ms. Blue didn't give you any sugar-coated half-truths. She assumed that as adults, these women could handle the realities of what faced them. If they couldn't, she intended to teach them how to do it.

Linking arms, the ladies continued their walk toward the church building. Lizzie loved these grounds. Visitors entering the church walked along a stone path leading from the parking lot to the back of the building. As the path continued up the sloping hill, a section of the walkway veered to the left away from the building. The second path climbed to an outdoor venue complete with gazebo, picnic tables, and playground. Outdoor luncheons took place here for events from birthday parties to baby dedications. Lizzie remembered playing on these stones with church friends after Sunday services. The stones sat at such a distance that it made them the perfect tool for a summer game of hopscotch. Many times the kids would steal a stick of chalk from the Sunday School room to create their board. The adults would often pretend to scold them for their illegal act. As an adult, Lizzie knew that in reality they were just thrilled that the kids wanted to stay after service to play on church grounds.

Lizzie howled, indulging herself in the first real laugh of the day. "I knew it! It was a plot!"

She gave them each a glance intended to appear displeased, knowing that they would see right through it. Despite her angst over participating in the evening, she was beginning to enjoy herself. It was sweet to find out that the ladies had worked together to get her here. Their feisty behavior reminded her that despite their age they weren't ready for the porch of the local senior home. The shared giggles of the three started coming together like the threads on a quilt as they made their way up the hill together.

"Of course we had a plot, sugar. Don't you think we can see when our girl is having troubles? We've been together longer than you've been alive, sugar. We know when one of our own needs help. And you, Lizzie, need some help," Blue said as she turned to give Lizzie a comedic look, complete with rolling eyes.

Blue was spot on, but Lizzie wasn't going to tell them that.

"I don't know why you think I'm so delicate. I'm fine. There's nothing wrong with me. I promise."

The pair walking with her came to a stop. Taking Lizzie's face into her aging hands, Abi looked deep into her young friend's eyes. "My dear, coming up on an anniversary like the death of your parents is enough to make anyone sad. It's normal. We're here for you."

Lizzie patted her surrogate grandmother's hands. She loved these women more than words could express.

"Yoo hoo!" sang a voice from the church door.

Claudia "Claud" Brown popped her head out of the church door. The fourth and final member of The Gals, she was the only one not native to the town. Coming into the group of friends later than the initial trio, an outsider would never know it from their relationships. Claud's husband Charlie was the older brother of Abi's husband Walter. Claud was a local girl who he met while he was a sailor in the US Navy stationed in Jacksonville. After the war, Charlie brought her back home to Everett Springs to marry and raise a family. She was immediately welcomed by her new sister-in-law and included in everything the friends did from that point on. A few years younger than the other ladies in the group, she became the little sister that none of them had. Though just as tough as her friends, Claud had a naive air about her that set her apart. It also happened to protect her from the sadness of life, making her the uplifting spirit in the group.

"Come on in! We're about ready to get started. Coats in the closet and drinks on the table. Grab a snack and let's begin. It's genealogy time, girls!" Claudia squeezed Lizzie a second time and then ushered her into the fellowship hall of the church. "Glad you're finally here, Lizzie, darling. I've missed you. You'll love it. I promise!"

After the quick hello, Claud was off to make sure everything was in order. Being the hostess of the group, she thrived on any kind of organized gathering. It was no wonder she was the one in charge of social events at the church. Lizzie remembered fondly the many birthday parties Claud arranged for her as a child. Each woman in the group had their own special strengths. Creating fabulous get-togethers was Claud's.

The First Baptist Church of Everett Springs was a historic, older building. One of the first churches in the area, it was built when the community was still in its infancy. The building saw many additions and renovations over the years, yet its sweet country charm still remained. Lizzie had attended this church from birth, making it a place of comfort to her. She knew the cracks and crevices of the building better than those in her own home.

Lizzie crossed the familiar room to put away her jacket. For some reason the evenings this fall were cooler than normal. Most days she welcomed the break from the south Georgia heat but the early occurrence made it a little unsettling this time.

I hope this isn't a bad omen, she thought.

Putting it out of her mind, she decided that she would have to learn to enjoy the state's crazy weather one day at a time. After all, it gave her an excuse to pull out the beautiful accent scarves that she loved so much. Lizzie stopped to bury her face deep into her lacy alpaca scarf. Its warm fiber felt like home. She couldn't help but smile.

"A good scarf can feel like a hug, can't it darlin'?" Blue placed her hand on Lizzie's face and smiled. She knew right away what Lizzie was thinking while standing in the entrance to the coat closet. With a wink and a smile, Blue floated out of the room as quietly as she had appeared.

Lizzie's mother had an astonishing creative ability. She could take a piece of tattered yarn and turn it into a beautiful accessory when you weren't even looking. Grace Hines was the one person the women of the church wanted to get as their Secret Sister partner at the annual women's retreat. She passed her love of fiber to Lizzie as a young girl. First, Grace had taught her to crochet. As her young fingers got caught in the yarn, Lizzie would beg to quit out of frustration. Grace was patient, just as her name suggested, and would show Lizzie one more time how to execute the troublesome stitch. Just before her death, Grace had begun teaching her daughter how to knit. Unfortunately, Lizzie wasn't meant to master that craft. She couldn't bring herself to pick up a pair of needles after losing her mother.

Lizzie hung up her coat and wound the scarf around the neck of the hanger. She picked up her worn leather messenger bag and headed toward the tables set up for the event. In preparation she had filled it with notebooks, pencils, and sticky notes. Coming prepared was her way of trying to toss an olive branch to her grandmother. Jack was right. She had to at least feign interest so that Grandma Tru could feel as though someone in the family would one day care for the work that she had done. Because their family was so small, that someone would have to be Lizzie whether she liked it or not.

As a child, Lizzie learned not raise her voice or run in the sanctuary of the church. It was for reserved, polite, and respectful behavior. It was appropriate for worship times and altar calls to get emotional. Hands could rise while the choir sang and the Spirit took hold, but it was not a place for childish exuberance. The Fellowship Hall was a different world for a Southern Baptist child. It was one of her favorite places. The hall was where events filled with dancing and laughter took place. Wedding receptions and baby showers built memories through unrestrained happiness and joy. It was the area where kids ran at birthday parties when the weather kept them from being outside. This space was meant for celebrations.

Lizzie stood looking around at the aged room. Though important, the hall wasn't gorgeous. A thick coat of old pale blue paint covered the cinder block walls. Secretly Lizzie always wondered if Miss Blue had something to do with that. Much to Blue's chagrin, this was one room that Tru was lobbying to change. She wanted to breathe happiness and joy into the space. Looking around, Lizzie could understand why. The dark brown carpet showed wear from years of use and carried the stains of red punch from celebrations past.

The Gals were the main cornerstones of the Tuesday Night Genealogy Gathering. The number of regular attenders was small, but each meeting usually saw a few additions from the congregation. Judging by the number of chairs available, it looked like there would be around fifteen coming tonight. It would be the perfect size for lively conversation while not being too intimidating for new attendees. As promised, Claud had set out a spread. A small table in the back presented bite-sized double chocolate brownies, salty pretzels to balance the sweets, and the same two drinks that showed up to every church function in the South: sweet tea and lemonade. The snacks and drinks were light by Claud's usual standards. Even though she was new to the group, Lizzie knew that you didn't have a lot of food or drink at a gathering like this. There were too many opportunities for accidental spills around valuable family history documents. Her grandmother would never stand for that.

Lizzie spied Gertrude setting up a display on a table in the front of the room.

"It looks like a decent turnout tonight, Gran. I guess I picked the right night to come."

"Hey there, sweetie. I'm so glad that you came!" Like always, Tru was her bubbly self. She gave her granddaughter a tight squeeze and then continued to arrange brochures and slips of paper on the table in front of her. "Are you looking forward to it?"

"You know what, Gran? I am. It took me a little bit to give in to your guerrilla tactics, but I think tonight will be fun." Lizzie smiled a big smile and hoped that her grandmother believed every word that she said.

"Jack made you promise to say that, didn't he?" Nothing slid past Gertrude Hines.

"Let's not split hairs. I'm here. That's all that matters, right?" Lizzie flashed a cheeky grin. She wasn't about to tell her grandmother that she was right. "Plus, I missed The Gals. It's been a few weeks since I've seen them all in the same place. I needed my old lady fix."

"You better watch yourself, Miss. These old ladies can still lick the likes of you. And, we'll do it in fabulous heels." Tru winked at her granddaughter. "Go sit your stuff down. You know the rules. No snacks at the table when documents are out. Have some brownies. Claud is all excited that she found a new recipe. Between you and me, it tastes exactly like the old recipe, but don't tell her that. It makes her happy. We'll be at this table over here." Tru pointed to a table in the front of the room to the left of the main display table that she was finishing. "Now, scoot. I've got to finish getting these brochures out. We're helping the local genealogy and historical societies make a push for volunteers. We need to clean up the old cemetery at the north end of town. It is starting to look a disgrace, and I will not have it deemed abandoned. If that happens it's a slippery slope. Some sleazy developer will come in and pave over our ancestors just so they can put in a big box warehouse company selling discount track suits and bulk jerky. Tacky. Just tacky."

"Now, Gran. Don't get yourself in a huff. You know your heart isn't as young as it used to be." Knowing that she had pushed it too far, Lizzie ducked and ran into the safe harbor of Blue and Abi who were standing just one table over. "Gals, save a girl, please!"

"You're on your own, sugar." Blue said. "We know where our bread is buttered, and it's with the old lady in the pinstriped pants right there." She pointed a brownie-filled hand in the direction of Gertrude. "We'll pack you up a lemonade for the road, though."

Lizzie couldn't help but laugh. "Here I thought you loved me."

"We do love you, dear. We're just more afraid of Tru than you," giggled a blushing Abi.

Gertrude threw a wadded up flier just right so it hit Abi in the back of the head.

"See? She fights back."

With that, the meeting was set to begin.

CHAPTER FOUR

The Tuesday Night Genealogy Gathering first started at Everett Springs First Baptist Church during the summer nights of the 1960s. The South is famous for its big kitchen tables and loud family meals. People share family stories as they pass the biscuits spurring on an interest in family history from a young age. During a fellowship meal after service one Sunday afternoon, the idea was born. The church women needed a genealogy club. The ladies already gathered together cooking for the congregation's usual events of marriages, births, and deaths. They took care of the elderly and ill. Their gatherings provided services that the church needed. It was worthwhile, but they wanted something else of their own that was just for fun.

In the beginning, the group met only once each month. Many of the women involved had young children at home that needed their attention. Over time, the casual monthly gathering turned into a regular weekly meet-up that discussed discovering family stories.

Lizzie stood still for a moment and just watched the movement throughout the room. Conversation buzzed as friends milled about saying their hellos and readying their materials for the meeting. Lizzie noticed an elderly man standing in the hallway that connected the hall to the main building. Thomas Abernathy was a tall, lanky man. His aged figure looked almost ghostlike from across the large room. As usual, his hands were busy completing a task, reaching and tugging at the objects before him. Lizzie couldn't tell what he was working on, but she could tell that he was struggling. She she set down her things and made her way over to see if she could help.

"Mr. Thomas, can I help you with that?"

"Well, hello, Miss Lizzie. Aren't you looking fine today? I'm just changing some light bulbs. I may be slow, but I'm determined. It will get done soon enough," he said with a chuckle.

Thomas was always polite. His gentle grace was a welcomed breeze for Lizzie. He reminded her of the stereotypical grandfather character seen in movies or television. His strong faith and moral compass was an example to all in the church, especially the younger generations. Pushing ninety years young, Thomas had known several generations of her family, including her great-grandfather. Though younger, she imagined him as a window into the generations of family that she hadn't met and another tie to her parents. He loved to share stories about them with Lizzie. Thomas' official role in the church was as deacon, but for years he had fancied himself its caretaker. He was the first man in and the last man out on a Sunday morning, even in his advanced age.

"Are you sure you don't need help? I don't mind. I like spending time with you, so you'd be doing me a favor." Lizzie meant every word. He was one of her favorite people in the community.

"No ma'am. You go on back to your meeting. Your granny will get at me if I give you any distraction from that group. She's put us all on notice. I might even get into trouble for talking to you. Don't you get me caught," Thomas giggled. He pretended to hide behind Lizzie so that Gertrude wouldn't see him. "Go on back to your group, darling. We'll catch up on Sunday."

Lizzie pretended to be as covert as possible in saying her goodbyes as she made her way back to the other side of the room as ordered. As she sat at the table chosen for her by Gertrude, she noticed that several small groups were beginning to gather over books and documents. Looking at each face, she noticed that most were widows just like her grandmother. Lizzie realized that these ladies weren't here just for the hobby; they were here for the companionship. Friends flitted from one table to another looking at the materials each brought to share during the meeting. Women grinned with pride as they pointed to documents and explained the stories associated with each item. They exchanged hugs and encouragement. It was a sweet sight, and one that Lizzie was happy to observe.

In the past, Gertrude had told her granddaughter stories of locating records at the local courthouse. Lizzie had never paid attention, or cared to ask, about the steps that it involved. As the other women gathered, she overheard stories of frustration over missing or damaged records. She listened as they shared their triumphs over missing pieces of information. They giggled and gave high-fives after finding out that a friend had proved a relationship discussed in family whispers. Lizzie found herself surprised at how interesting it was to listen to these ladies. It felt almost magical as mysteries cracked wide open in front of her. They weren't discussing her family tree but she still found it compelling.

"I cannot tell Gran this is interesting", Lizzie said as she shook her head and stifled a laugh.

Blue pulled a chair up to the table and sat down next to Lizzie. "Tru can go sit over there with Abi. You're mine tonight, sugar." Blue patted her on the leg and settled in to listen to the meeting introduction.

This meeting wasn't about a specific topic such as a repository in the area or researching a certain type of record as many meetings were. Tonight the group decided to discuss the care and keeping of the special items that every family historian hoped to find. They brought out the Holy Grail of family history: family Bibles, photographs, and journals.

Sitting next to her at the table, Blue pulled a small leather-bound book out of her bag that sat at the corner of the table. Lizzie couldn't tell if it was a Bible or a diary, but it looked old. The cover of the book was worn, and the bottom edge of the spine looked as though it had spent many years on a shelf. The leather was creased and broken in various places indicating either advanced age or regular use. Small, thin strips of leather cord wound around the book to keep it closed.

Lizzie wondered what secrets the bound pages held. Before she had too much time to daydream, her grandmother called the room to order.

"Okay, girls. Let's all get focused. Time to stop trading research stories and get started sharing those treasures!"

Gertrude was in full leader mode. Lizzie loved seeing her grandmother take control of a room. Immediately she directed everyone's attention to a stack of brochures that she had sitting on the main table. She pointed a graceful hand to the display she had spent so much time organizing when Lizzie first arrived.

"Before we get started, I want to make sure that you notice the brochures here for our upcoming service project. The old town cemetery north of here is in bad shape. I'm sure most of you have kinfolk amongst those graves just like Lizzie and I do," Gertrude gestured toward her granddaughter. "Many of us are concerned over the lack of care it is receiving. You may not know, but once a cemetery closes to new burials, which this one is, it runs the risk of being deemed abandoned. If that happens, the city is then free to transfer ownership of the property. This can lead to all sorts of trouble for those buried there who no longer have identified family to step up and protect them. It's up to us as the keepers of their history and stories to make sure this doesn't happen. Many have already pledged time and supplies in our efforts. What I need from you tonight is your voice. If you are interested in helping me reach out to the other historical and genealogical groups in the tri-county area you can sign up on the sheet provided. Oh, and take some brochures with you. Litter them everywhere you go so we can get the word out."

"It's not litter if it serves a purpose," muttered Blue with a wink to Lizzie.

"Moving on to current business," Gertrude continued with a stern eye pointed toward her life-long friend. "Tonight my granddaughter, Lizzie has joined us. Let's show her how exciting family history can be! While we're sharing tonight, let's talk about where you found your prize and how you're caring for it now. Who wants to start?" Finishing her call to order, Gertrude conceded the floor to the first member holding a family Bible.

Those in attendance reached into archival boxes and research bags to pull out the examples that they brought to share. It struck Lizzie just how similar they all looked to her kids at the center. The ladies all wiggled in their seats with their hands in the air as if waiting for their turn during Show and Tell.

Some days we're all still kids inside, she thought.

During the meeting, Lizzie enjoyed hearing stories of lost photos tucked into odd places and documents found folded into books long forgotten. With each item, the group discussed appropriate archival procedures. They seemed to all agree on the proper way to store and display vintage photographs. Yet tempers flared when the discussion turned to the use of linen gloves when handling materials. At times the room seemed to be one hair shy of an argument. Lizzie never realized that genealogy could come so close to being a contact sport.

Despite hearing their interesting stories, Lizzie couldn't keep her mind from wondering about the small leather book on the table in front of Blue. Finally her wait was over, thought Lizzie, as Blue started moving her chair in what she thought was an effort to stand in front of the group. To her disappointment, all her friend did was shift her body so that she was sitting in a more comfortable position.

Lizzie had to know the secrets that Blue held in that tiny aged package. The longer she looked upon it the stronger the desire grew. She couldn't head home without knowing what was behind the cover even if she didn't understand why.

"Blue, honey, you haven't told us your story. Don't you want to share your book?" Lizzie asked sweetly.

"Oh, darlin', this isn't mine. It's your grandmother's."

Blue's words took Lizzie by complete surprise. Before she could regain her thoughts, Gertrude was again addressing the group.

"Several years ago, I was going through some boxes that we had packed up after Daddy passed away. Those boxes had been up in the attic for, oh goodness me, almost two decades untouched. Among other papers, I found this diary. I had never known that my father was one to write his thoughts, and by the contents, it's pretty clear that he didn't intend on me knowing it. Well, not until his death." Gertrude walked over to the table and picked up the diary. She held it gently against her chest.

Lizzie realized how emotional sharing the diary must have been for her grandmother. She couldn't recall another time when Gertrude was so soft spoken.

"Gran, I never knew that you had this," whispered Lizzie.

"Well, dear, there's a reason. This diary holds some important but difficult pieces of history. It also holds some secrets that I'm sure my father didn't want the whole town to know. I think it's time now. Since we're talking about protecting the items we discover, I want to ask a question of everyone in the room. What happens if you find something the original individual may not have wanted to stand the test of time? How do you handle the sensitive information that you come across in your research?" Gertrude tossed the question out to the room. Only half listening to the discussion, Lizzie sat in shock wondering why her grandmother had kept this secret from her.

"What on earth is inside that diary?" said Lizzie.

Claud was the first to answer. "Well, I suppose it's something that you need to really think upon. For me, if the creator kept it hidden, who are we to make it public? Perhaps we should respect their wishes."

"Oh, don't be so nervous about it, Claud," answered Blue. "I say get it out into the light. Rip back the curtains. Secrets are only dangerous in the dark. You've got to expose the monster to slay it."

Abi, as usual, tried to bridge the gap between the two ladies who stood on opposite ends of the discussion. "Both have valid points. I think that the protection of individual privacy is the main concern in a situation like this. Are those involved still alive? If they have passed you must look at the immediate descendant for that answer. If they give the go-ahead, then shine light on the secret and take away its power just as Blue said."

"That's exactly what I did," said Gertrude. "Since this is my father's diary, I know that the individual in question is no longer living. I also know that the other individuals also listed in the diary have passed as well. I am his only living child, so the decision falls to me. Well, to me and to Lizzie." She grinned with pride as she gestured toward her granddaughter who was finally in attendance.

Lizzie felt drained. The revelation that her grandmother held a diary filled with emotional and difficult family secrets was almost too much to take in. Her imagination had spent the better part of the evening dreaming up fantastic scenarios for the diary. Each scenario had one important thing in common: it was supposed to be Blue's family story not her own. Now that she was adding her family to the fantasy she wasn't sure if she wanted to know the truth.

Without much prompting, the conversation began to wind down as the late hour approached. Several other women added their opinions on the importance of privacy versus discovery, but most concurred with Abi. Many commented that they were glad for the opportunity to discuss something of a serious nature as a group. Once finished, they began gathering their materials and started saying goodnight to dear friends. Lizzie had already planned on staying behind to help her grandmother and The Gals clean up the Fellowship Hall. Now it would take a team of Clydesdales to drag her from the church. She had to get her hands around that diary - and her grandmother's neck. As the ladies milled around the coat room gathering their belongings, Lizzie looked for Gertrude.

"Gran, can we talk about this diary for a minute?" Lizzie whispered. She tried to act as if she was patient and not at all intrigued.

"Genealogy isn't so boring now, is it?" Gertrude giggled as she packed up her display board and brochures. "This is just the beginning, dear."

After the others had left, The Gals gathered around a central table making sure that everyone had a seat as well as a full view of the diary. Finally, the important conversation would start.

"Gran, why didn't you tell me about this sooner?" asked Lizzie.

"Sweetheart, I didn't realize you'd be as interested as you are in your great-grandfather's diary. I apologize. I thought bringing it out on your first gathering would get your attention, but I didn't think it would upset you. It was just a little bait for the hook. I guess I was right, wasn't I!" Gertrude slid the bound book across the table to Lizzie. "Go ahead. Take a peek."

Lizzie reached across the table for the diary. "Why do I feel as though you're a drug dealer hoping to start my addiction?"

"My stars! Why do you have to be so crass sometimes?"

Lizzie knew it was serious if her grandmother started scolding her, so she decided to focus on the information in front of her. She wasn't sure herself why she was so desperate to know the secrets of the little book. Once she felt the weight of it in her hands, Lizzie wasn't sure that she was ready to open it. The diary itself was heavier than she thought. What if the contents were heavier as well?

"Do you know what's inside?" Lizzie asked with trepidation.

"Yes, I do," answered Gertrude. "I read it on my own, and then I took it to The Gals. We've all looked through it. It was part of me deciding what to do with the diary. Finally, just as Blue said, we decided that it needed to come into the light so that the secrets could no longer hold power or fear. The words written on these pages make it clear that they held a great deal of both over my father. You're old enough to consult with now, so we're inviting you into our secret."

"You're not asking me for a blood oath are you? Blue better not have a knife hidden up her sleeve."

"Don't worry, sugar. I killed the chicken yesterday. You're in the clear," Blue said with nary a smile or laugh.

"Oh, Blue. I do swear," gasped Claud.

Rolling her eyes, Gertrude continued, "I just want you to be prepared, sweetheart. As you read it, you should remember that these times were different. This diary will contain some things that are upsetting to you because they contradict your understanding of how we are to live. Are you sure that you're ready to unlock that door?"

"Gran, I think I can handle it." Lizzie was a little offended that her grandmother needed to ask these questions. After all, she was thirty-two years old. She had dealt with the deaths of both parents at the young age of twelve. She could handle anything as an adult.

"Well, then. By all means, take a peek." Gertrude leaned back into her chair and crossed her legs. She sipped on her sweet tea and portrayed a cool exterior to match her granddaughter's attitude.

"Welcome to the club," said Blue. "Let's just hope you know what you're getting yourself into."

CHAPTER FIVE

Lizzie held the diary in her hands. It was surprisingly heavy for a book of its size. She turned it over, looking at the binding.

"Well, let's not take all night, sugar," said Blue. "We're not the youngest chickens in the coop. We might just all die of old age before you get to the good stuff."

Abi swatted her friend while the others laughed.

"Go on, dear. It's time you started reading," said Gertrude.

With Gran's permission, Lizzie removed the straps from the body of the journal. She peeled back the front cover in slow motion and smoothed the aged paper. The front page was starting to fade into a warm brown much like the tea they were sipping.

The first blank page of the diary revealed a personal statement in the handwriting of her great-grandfather, Alston James.

"Into this diary I've poured my heart and deeds.
I beg understanding from the next generation,
May God forgive me and have mercy on my soul.

~ Alston James, amended in 1979."

Lizzie's heart raced. Why would her great-grandfather need mercy? What secret could lie beyond these pages? She inhaled a slow, deep breath before turning the next page.

She could already feel that her life was changing.

***

The Diary of Alston James: 21 August 1934

My heart is heavy today. I feel as though I have no one to turn to in this situation. Lacking counsel, I pour my thoughts here in the hopes that it will bring clarity. I fear that I have stumbled onto something that would be devastating to our family if it were discovered by the wrong person.

My sweet sister, what have you done?

The fear I have for her, for us all, is overwhelming. She has stepped outside the boundaries of acceptable behavior as dictated by society with no regard to the consequences. If the wrong people discover her secret, she'll end up in the grave. I must protect her, but I don't know how to do so. I don't even know if I should. This will surely break the hearts of our parents.

My sister is so young and innocent. She doesn't understand. This world has consequences whether we want to believe in them or not. The men in town will not ignore this. It's as if she's throwing dirt in their faces.

How on earth am I to protect her?

As a child, Alston James was determined to be more than a farmer. Like his father, generations of men in the James family ended up in the fields. Not Alston. He longed for the easy life in town just like many of the other men in his graduating class at South Georgia Teachers College. A man of consistency, he often created goals and continued toward them in a slow and steady fashion. He didn't enjoy deviating from his outlined path, so he made the perfect student. Trustworthy, dependable, and predictable in every way, Alston reached his goal and graduated as part of the Class of 1932.

After finishing his education, he returned home to marry his high school sweetheart, Anne Varney. Both were children of farmers who shared the same dream of an easier future than their past. They longed for a life that wasn't covered with red dirt and dust from the fields. Almost immediately he joined the staff of the local high school, and the newlyweds had the home that they had always wanted.

In 1934, their lives changed.

Although Alston loved teaching in the classroom, his main love was working with wood. Sharing this practical yet artistic craft with his students became his focus. Within two years, Alston became known throughout the community for his skill with both the wood and the students in his classroom. His younger sister often teased him that as hard as he tried, he was still covered in the dust that he had tried to escape from the family farm. Alston knew that the main reason she liked to tease him was because he would react and respond, so he always obliged.

His favorite time of the day was when Eliza would stop by his shop to visit. Many times they would leave the school together after classes finished for the day. Although there was a six-year age difference between them, spending this time together every day kept them close as siblings. Many times Eliza would spend her weekends in town with her brother and his wife. Alston and Anne counted the time they spent with her a blessing. They each dreamed of a time when perhaps Eliza would move to town to start her own family, keeping them all together.

Lately Eliza hadn't been stopping by her brother's classroom after school. He had noticed changes in her behavior. She no longer wanted to spend free afternoons walking through town shops with her sister-in-law. They didn't know why things had shifted in her personality and behavior, and they weren't enjoying the changes.

Today, Alston decided to wander the halls of Everett Springs High School in search of his absentee sibling. The school was quieting down as students made their way towards home. Alston walked through the main hallway hearing nothing but the sounds of his own shoes. He peered around doors and into classrooms to see if his sister was sitting in discussion with another instructor. Unfortunately, he found no signs of where she may have been.

"The library," Alston whispered.

Eliza was an avid reader. Although, they couldn't afford many books, his parents stressed the importance of reading. They saved advertisements, labels from seed bags, or newspaper articles for their children to read after school. Each turned into a story at bedtime or around the dinner table. They created games that encouraged their wild imaginations and creativity. Alston considered his mother a master storyteller, not unlike P.L. Travers. His mother had little faith in her talent. She didn't believe that a woman in the Deep South could have a career writing children's stories in the 1930s. She also believed in conforming to the expectations of society, and she taught her children to do so as well. They could bend the bonds of status and class, but they couldn't break them without feeling the sting of being different. Some changes needed to come only with the passage of time.

The talent of Mrs. James showed in the minds and imaginations of her children, especially Eliza. During on one their afternoon walks, Eliza shared her dream was to leave Everett Springs. She wanted to ride a train to New York where she was sure she could be an author. She fancied herself the American Dorothy L. Sayers or Agatha Christie. While Alston and Anne wanted her to have dreams of living in Everett Springs, Eliza had dreams of being bigger than her home town. She wanted to move to a bigger city in a new part of the country where she couldn't be limited by small towns and small minds. She had dreams of the life that she saw in newsreels and picture shows. Eliza James wanted to be cosmopolitan.

Alston reached the school library and opened the door with great care and respect. Although he was a teacher, he was still one of the youngest members on staff. It was difficult for him to remember that he was no longer a student bound to the rules of his childhood. In contrast, he was a teacher who could now help determine and enforce those rules. This time his quiet entry worked to his advantage allowing him to see what may have otherwise stayed hidden.

Peering around the heavy wooden door into the dark-filled library, Alston reeled back in shock. Hidden between two shelves of books was his youngest sister, Eliza, and she wasn't alone.

He couldn't see his sister's face, but he recognized her clothing immediately. After a summer's afternoon with a Harper's Bazaar, Eliza became convinced that she had to own a dress just like Bette Davis modeled on the cover. It would be her first step toward creating a style like career women in the Big Apple. By selling eggs and baked goods in town, their mother saved the money to buy the fabric needed to make her daughter's dream come true. The straight skirt with a pleated bottom teased Alston as he stood there unable to find the words to shout out to his sister. He tried to adjust his eyes to the low light to see who accompanied her but the angle and location of the bookcase prevented it. The young man's face may have been hidden, but

Alston saw one important detail. Two dark-skinned hands wrapped around his sister's waist.

Alston started toward the couple. At the same time, the doors to the library flung open creating a loud racket. Two of the school's football players entered laughing. The distraction caused Alston to turn his attention toward the door and away from his sister. By the time he looked again at the library's stacks he realized he had been too late. The voices of the players caught Eliza's attention, too.

His sister and her companion were gone.

CHAPTER SIX

After reading the diary's opening entry, Lizzie needed to read more. She flipped through the diary's pages looking for an answer to the problem that plagued her great-grandfather. Patience wasn't her strong suit, and there was no use in pretending she had it now.

"Lizzie, darlin', you need to go through this diary one entry at a time. Don't go looking too far ahead. If you search for an answer before you even know the story you'll cause the truth to become lost," Gertrude cautioned.

"Gran, what's going on here? I didn't even know that your father had a sister much less that she was somehow attached to a scandal in the family."

"Daddy did have a younger sister. It tortured him to talk about her, so we didn't much. Her name was Eliza, just like you."

"Whoa. Wait just a second," said Lizzie as she stood in surprise, causing the chair to wobble behind her. Raising her hands in the air, she took a step back from the table. "What do you mean her name was Eliza?

Was I named after your aunt? No one thought I might want to know this before now?"

"We don't need you getting all riled up, sister." Blue slid out a chair and patted its back as encouragement for Lizzie to take a seat. "Do your Gran's old heart good and sit down." It may have sounded like a request, but Lizzie knew it was the only polite order she was going to get from Blue if she continued to pace the room.

"We all knew about it, dear. We were just waiting until your grandmother thought the time was right," whispered Abi. "Sweetheart, just listen to her for a minute before you get all twisted into knots."

Gertrude crossed her hands in her lap and took in a calming breath before starting the conversation over. "My father always spoke of his sister with such adoration. He loved her. She was his baby sister. It was his responsibility to protect her, and he took that charge to heart. Growing up I knew that she had an accident at a young age, but I wasn't sure exactly what it was or when it had occurred. It was painful for him to discuss because he felt as if he was responsible. The only way he knew how to cope was to keep it locked up, so we didn't talk about her often. It just opened too many wounds, I suppose. I always had the feeling that whatever happened was something that we didn't need to dwell on so I didn't push. It wasn't until years later that I learned her story."

Emotions of the past began to crawl cross Gertrude's face. Her life-long friends reached for her. Abi leaned in for a hug as Blue reached for Gertrude's hand. Claud whispered prayers under her breath much to Blue's irritation.

"I don't know much about her outside of the diary, but he did tell me of her beauty and grace. Her full name was Eliza Gertrude James. I am the bearer of her middle name. When you were born, you were such a beautiful baby that her name just came to mind. You held the beauty that my father talked about when he thought of his sister. Your parents loved it, so Eliza you became. It's a name that connects us to each other as well as to the past."

Gertrude watched Lizzie's face as she took it all in. Her big green eyes were even larger than normal as she soaked in the conversation. It was only when Lizzie dropped her eyes to look at the diary that she knew it was time to continue talking about its secrets.

"You look like you have some questions," Gertrude said. "Where do you want to start?"

Lizzie wasn't sure how to answer her grandmother. Thoughts raced through her head as she sat looking at the diary. All she expected from this evening was a boring night at church to appease her grandmother. One small collection of dusty paper had changed everything. Lizzie knew that conversations of the past could be painful. She wasn't sure that she wanted to open another wound over a woman she didn't even know existed until a few moments earlier.

"I just discovered that my namesake is a mysterious aunt that we don't discuss. I have a lot of questions. What did she do? Why was your father so concerned with her dating a boy that he cut her out of his life like that?"

"It was a little more complicated than that. It was a different time. People saw things differently then. You'll have to read the diary to understand."

Lizzie rubbed her temples. Her life had always felt like it had a shadow over it. People always looked at her like she was different. She always assumed it was her pain over her parents' death that made them uncomfortable. Now she wondered if there was something else complicating matters. What kind of scandal did her great aunt cause? Immediately she felt like blaming Eliza Gertrude James, bearer of both beauty and shame.

"I only wanted to come to the meeting for a few hours to make you happy, Gran. I had no idea a family scandal was waiting on me."

Blue took control of the conversation. "Listen here. You need to take a breath before you blow a gasket. That won't be something pretty, and I don't feel like putting you together tonight. It's been a long day, and I don't have the energy." She rose to get a snack tray that was still sitting on the dessert table. "Lemon square?"

Claud broke from her prayers as the tray came within inches of her nose. "How on earth can you be thinking of sweets during a conversation like this, Blue?"

"Easy. They're here. I'm staring at them. What's not to understand?" Blue popped a small yellow confection into her mouth and returned to her chair with a flourish and a wink at Claud. She took her role as the grounding force of the group seriously, even if it did come out of her mouth in a mixture of bluntness and comedy.

"Honestly, Blue," Abi said. "The diary holds all the answers, honey. It's a heavy story, but it isn't your story. It just might teach you a thing or two. The past tends to do that if you let it."

"I'm sure it's interesting, but I don't see what I can learn from a dusty book written by a man I didn't know in an era I didn't live. I don't see how it's connected," Lizzie said.

"Sometimes you struggle with making peace over the events of your past." Gertrude paused. "I - no, we - thought it would be helpful for you to see how others dealt with difficulty in their lives. Sometimes the past is painful, but other times it can bring perspective. I want you to see how my father and his family dealt with difficult times in the hopes that it helps you deal with yours."

"That is part of why we are drawn to study our family history," Claud added. "It helps us put what we're dealing with today into perspective."

"In some cases, the strength of our ancestors helps us move past something that's holding us down," said Abi.

"Or, in the case of my aunt, their struggles teach us how to let go before our troubles destroy us."

Lizzie looked at the diary once again. Picking it up, she flipped through the pages being careful not to damage the aging book. Words flashed through in pieces as she moved through the time line of events left behind by her great-grandfather. Curious, she started to linger over an entry partway through the diary.

Her grandmother interrupted her focus by placing a hand on top of the text, limiting Lizzie from going further. She couldn't help but notice how gently her grandmother's hand rested on the diary. For a moment, it reminded Lizzie of the gentleness with which she raised Lizzie. It wasn't a figure of speech when Lizzie talked of her grandmother ruling with an iron fist of grace. It was all true. Her grandmother could both take control and induce calm all at the same time. She was doing it again now.

"Gran, I thought you wanted me to read the diary to learn the great family secret that is lost in its pages. You keep giving me these teasers of information but then stop me short. That can't possibly be playing by the rules."

"I'm making the rules, and the first is to take it one page at a time. You have to read it in order. Understand that my father and his sister lived in a different time. The experiences that they had were guided by the rules of society, and those rules varied from the ones that steady us today. It's dark, so you need to prepare yourself. It will be hard, but it will be worth it. Knowing how these events affected our family will help you as you face your own demons, just like Abi and Claud said. Just remember that we're all with you every step of the way."

Lizzie glanced at her watch and was shocked at the time. The Tuesday Night Genealogy Gathering had ended over an hour earlier. It was time to head home to Jack. She wanted time to get his questions about the evening out of the way before it got much later. Lizzie didn't dread sharing the events of the evening, but she didn't want it to delay her from beginning the diary. As she started gathering her things, she picked up the journal and held it close to her chest. It was hard to believe that such a small object could cause such a stir.

"I hear you, Gran," started Lizzie. "I don't quite understand why you think after all these years I need to focus on working through what happened to Mama and Daddy. I've already done that. The memories just creep up once in a while."

Lizzie felt like all eyes at the table were on her. She didn't understand why this family of friends thought she was their latest project. Didn't they have dead people to chase?

"I'm fine. I promise," Lizzie said with great exasperation.

"My dear child, you are as fine as a piece of antique china. We just don't want to see you break like it," said Blue with a squeeze. "Grab your scarf and jacket. I'll walk you out."

Lizzie couldn't help but laugh. Once again Blue had managed to bring a smile to her face.

Lizzie began to make the rounds with hugs and compliments for a lovely evening. As she was saying goodbye, she couldn't help but realize how blessed she was to have these ladies in her life. They were as special to her as her grandmother, and each represented a different piece of her personality.

Blue gave her a wink that was as familiar to Lizzie as the hugs that often followed. It was a hint that everything was going to be all right.

"Let's go, kiddo," she said.

Abi, rose to give her a hug. Holding Lizzie tight, she whispered, "Call me tonight if you want to talk about what you read. I just know that you're not going to wait until tomorrow." Lizzie could always count on her to be there when she needed a sounding board for her thoughts.

"You know I will, Miss Abi," said Lizzie.

"Not before she calls me," said Gertrude with a smile.

Claud reached out for Lizzie's hand. Pulling her close, she gave her the warmest smile that she could muster. "I packed you a snack for the road. It would go well with a warm cup of tea as you read." Claud always thought of the hospitable thing to do, and Lizzie knew that if not for any reason but this woman she would never go hungry.

Gertrude walked toward her granddaughter. "You have no idea how much it meant to me that you joined us tonight. I am so glad that I can finally share this family secret with you. Knowing that you might have interest in our family's history is thrilling. It's sharing what I love best with who I love best." Gertrude gave Lizzie a hug and a kiss on the cheek. Holding her by the shoulders, she looked at Lizzie for a moment and smiled. "Let's meet at the park for lunch tomorrow. Under your favorite tree?"

"I'd love it as much as I love you," Lizzie said. A simple act of saying goodnight to these four special women made her feel blessed.

"You know I love you gals, right?"

Wrapping an arm around Lizzie's shoulder, Blue piped up. "Darlin', of course you do. We didn't give you any other choice."

Lizzie and Blue left the church leaving the remaining three friends to close up the Fellowship Hall.

"Do you think we need to pray for her?" asked Claud.

"I think she's in for the biggest ride of her life," replied Gertrude. "She'll see that pain and distress that can happen to any family. Her life has been tough, but there is so much more beyond what happened to her parents. I hope the diary shows her that she has to let go or it will destroy her. It's going to be a tough ride for that child."

Abi patted her friend's hand. "Let's hope she listens. Let the healing begin."

CHAPTER SEVEN

During the drive home, Lizzie was able to calm down and allow her mind to wander through the events of the evening. Besides a mysterious aunt, she had inherited a diary that held scandal and intrigue. It was better than finding a new novel at the library, and it involved her family. It was quite interesting, even if she wouldn't admit it to her grandmother. She couldn't wait to get home and throw herself into the diary again. Lizzie needed to discover the secret that her Grandfather Alston hid away so long ago.

As Lizzie pulled into the driveway, she noticed a faint glow of light coming from the back porch. She knew immediately that Jack had lit a fire in the brick pit. Lizzie could see right through his plot. Her loving husband would present it as a romantic gesture but Lizzie knew the truth. Jack had waited outside so they could talk about the events of the evening. Lizzie maneuvered the vehicle into its parking spot and made her way toward the house.

"Hey, girl. Back here," hollered Jack.

Lizzie rounded the small wooden fence that separated the side yard from the back of the house. She loved watching the sun rise from the side porch, but the brick patio in the backyard was her favorite place to spend time in the evenings. Sitting in front of the fire pit, Jack made himself comfortable on the glider that they kept for nights just like this. It was in the perfect position. The glider sat close enough to the fire to enjoy its warmth but far enough back that Lizzie needed to snuggle deep into Jack's arms if she wanted to stay warm on a chilly night.

"It's feeling kind of airish." Lizzie chucked over her grandmother's usual description for cool evenings.

Lizzie was glad that Jack had chosen this spot to welcome her home. Seeing him in the glow of the firelight reminded her that she was a lucky woman. His strong jaw line and wispy hair stood out even in the dim light. Jack had become more handsome as he aged. Dropping her bags by the back door, she met him on the patio, giving him a kiss before sitting down next to him.

Jack handed her a warm cup of cider that he had waiting on her.

"Gran must have called you after I left the church."

"Could be," Jack said with a smirk. "So, was it awful? Did they torture you? Were there dead people there?"

"It was an uneventful evening," she said, "except for the zombie that ate the last lemon square. Miss Claud was ticked." Lizzie was glad that Jack couldn't see her face clearly in the dim light because her smile would have given her away.

Jack leaned his head back against the cushion of the glider and laughed deep from his core. "Try telling me the truth this time."

"Only if you don't say 'I told you so'," Lizzie said. "It was great. I didn't realize how much I had missed spending time with those gals. I loved seeing them together, and of course Miss Blue was in rare form. Gran fought dirty."

"Not Miss Gertrude! Never."

"She was sneaky. She even gave me a bribe to keep coming back."

Lizzie set her cider down on the cedar side table as she got up from the glider. Making her way back to her bags next to the door, she called over her shoulder, "Hey, did you know they were giving me the diary tonight?"

"I may have known something about a little bribery. As a deputy of the law I can claim no part of it. I was just an innocent party to the plotting. I take no blame and accept no responsibility." Jack raised his glass and winked.

Blue. Lizzie knew that sneaky old lady had a hand in the planning, but Jack's wink sealed it.

Returning with the diary, Lizzie sat down on the glider. Turning sideways to face her husband, she crossed her legs and leaned toward the glow of the fire to look at the diary. Jack stared at his wife. Seeing her happy brought a smile to his face.

"Gran sent me home with her father's diary, which you knew was going to happen."

"I may have suspected something like that," replied Jack as he stretched his legs out, crossing his feet on top of the ledge that surrounded the fire pit.

"Did you know about my aunt, Eliza Gertrude?"

"When I was talking to Miss Gertrude she gave me a little information on the diary, but she didn't give me many details. She was an aunt, then?"

"Yes, she was my great-aunt," Lizzie answers. "As it turns out, she was the woman for whom we are both named. I suppose she was also the first Lizzie. Aunt Eliza also had a secret. It's intriguing. It seems that she did something that convinced my Grandfather Alston that harm would come to her or to the family. The second entry alluded to what might be a hidden affair. He caught her meeting a man."

"Oh, so your great-aunt was a trollop. A ne'er do well. A woman of ill repute."

Lizzie swatted at Jack's arm. He tried to recoil from the blow but wasn't successful.

"Hey, I'm her namesake. I'd ask you to be more respectful, sir." Lizzie giggled in response. She knew he was just trying to nag her. It was working.

"Yes, ma'am. I'll note that for the future. Be respectful," Jack teased. "You seem much happier than before you left. You enjoyed yourself, didn't you?"

"I did, surprisingly enough. It was interesting to hear the other ladies talk of their family stories. I can see why Gran loves her meetings so much. I don't know that I'll end up being as involved as Gran, but I think I should spend more time asking her questions about her research. Especially about this diary...." Lizzie's voice trailed off as she looked down at the small book she held in her hands. It felt so heavy, yet so delicate at the same time.

"What are you thinking, Lizzie?"

"I'm anxious to dig into the story of Eliza and see how it ends. Gran mentioned being eaten up by our demons. I'm sure it isn't anything like my mind is suggesting, but it is interesting to imagine. The young man wasn't one they allowed her to date at the time, but I'm not sure of much else. What if it was a clandestine affair of star-crossed lovers that tore a family apart?"

"You want her to be your family's version of Juliet." Jack smiled at his wife. It thrilled him to see her getting so excited. With the fall coming around, she had been a quieter, more subdued version of the girl he loved. It was such a sad time for her, and she deserved this type of joy every day. "I'll be your Romeo, you know." Jack leaned in to sneak a kiss.

"You are a hopeless romantic, Mr. Clydell." Lizzie leaned in to kiss her husband, meeting him with a smile.

"Why, yes, I am, Mrs. Clydell. Now finish telling me about this secret diary."

"That's all there is to tell right now. Alston began writing it in 1934. That's all I know."

"How old was his Eliza during all of this? She must have been a younger sister, right?"

"Aunt Eliza was in high school at the time. I need to ask Gran what she knows of her, but I would suspect that she was at least fifteen years old. She couldn't have been too old. It's just occurred to me that I don't know much about my family's past. I feel bad that I never asked about it before. I guess that was Gran's goal with this diary, wasn't it?"

"That and she wants you to finally understand that you are more than what troubles you each fall into. I understand it, Lizzie, I really do, but it casts such a shadow over you. It's time for you to understand that it's okay to be sad, but it's also okay to move forward and live. That's what your grandmother is trying to teach you. The world moves on. You don't have to be sad to remember your parents."

Lizzie bristled at her husband's honesty. She knew that Jack was right, but she didn't see what the two had to do with each other at all.

"I'm trying. I am. I just don't understand why we have to keep talking about it."

Jack switched gears back to the place where Lizzie was happy. "Let's go back to the diary. I bet you're glad that you'll be home from work tomorrow. Should I expect a full report when I'm done with my shift?"

"You know it. This is going to be a good story. I just don't understand what could have caused my great-grandfather to erase his sister from our family."

"There's only one way to find out. Read the diary."

Jack was right. They could sit and discuss it all night, but it was all speculation at this point. Lizzie decided to head to bed with her antique diary and sink deep into the mind of Alston James. As she was carrying her mug of warm cider up the stairs to the bedroom, her cell phone rang.

"Lizzie, dear, don't you have that diary around your mug tonight. You leave it downstairs."

"How did you know I had a mug of cider, Gran?" Lizzie giggled. Leave it to her grandmother to catch her in the act.

"I know because I am the all-powerful Gran. Plus, Jack told me earlier that he was going to have a fire and some cider waiting on you in case you needed to talk. That's neither here nor there. Now, go on to bed. Just don't have drinks around my Daddy's diary or I'll swat you."

"I promise. I'm walking into the kitchen right now. Anything else you'd like to order, I mean, suggest?"

"Yes. Don't call Abi first. It's my father's diary. I get to hear all about it before that old woman does."

"Goodnight, Gran."

"Goodnight, dear."

Lizzie left her cider on the kitchen counter like an obedient granddaughter and headed up the stairs once again. It was time to find what mysterious events the diary held inside its covers.

***

Lizzie pulled her hair into a loose bun and crawled between the crisp white sheets of their queen-sized bed. Closing her eyes, she took a minute to enjoy the warmth and weight of the quilts on her legs. She scooted her body into the curves of the mattress from years of sleeping in the same place. Rather than complaining that they needed a new mattress, Lizzie took comfort in it. Knowing that there was one spot in this world molded just for her made her smile. The dip in the mattress had become one of her favorite places in the house.

A smile came across her face as she smoothed the wrinkles from the quilts. Now that arthritis plagued her hands, Gertrude turned to a sewing machine for her quilting. Before that, Gertrude preferred to create her quilts by hand in the fashion of her mother and grandmother. Lizzie loved that it was a talent that her grandmother liked to share by gifting the quilts at Christmas and birthdays. They took her back to her childhood. From the time she was a child, these same homemade quilts kept Lizzie's beds warm at night. They comforted her while she was sick, and they gave structure to imaginative forts. It seemed so fitting to Lizzie that even now as a grown woman in her own home, the quilts would once again be part of her next adventure.

Perfect for reading, she thought as her mind moved back to the contents of the diary.

Lizzie reached over to her bedside table and lifted the leather-bound diary from its resting place. Opening the cover she read once again the dedication:

"In this diary I poured my heart and deeds.
I beg forgiveness from the next generation,
May God have mercy on my soul.

~ Alston James, amended in 1979."

"Didn't you die in 1979?" Lizzie made a mental note to ask her grandmother about it when they met for lunch the following afternoon. She couldn't recall the details surrounding his death. It seemed strange that he worried about his diary so close to the end of his life. Turning the pages, Lizzie sank into the diary. "Let's see what secrets you were keeping, Gramps."

***

Diary of Alston James: 23 August 1934

I've been watching my sister closely over the last few days. I realized that I need to prove my suspicions. I couldn't allow myself to jump to conclusions. I needed to learn more about what we were facing.

I haven't been able to find her in the library again. She must be meeting her companion at a different location. It couldn't have been easy for him to slip into the school - too dangerous for her to go to the colored school, too.

Watching her with that boy was just so shocking. I never would have suspected her of something like this.

Today I decided to follow her after she left the high school. Instead of walking toward home, she took the east road out of town. We never walk along the east road…

Eliza seemed completely at ease. I don't think she suspected that I was looking for her.

I saw her slip into a barn out at the old Atkinson place. I called her name just before she went inside, but she didn't hear me. Either I was too far away or the words just didn't leave my lips as loud as I thought.

Eliza looked over her shoulder, but I think it was just out of caution. She didn't seem to see me at all.

I saw through the window that they were talking, and their familiarity showed a relationship that isn't just a friendship. I took a deep breath to steady myself and waited until they had turned their backs.

Just as I was about to enter the barn, I saw what I dreaded. He took Eliza, my baby sister, into his arms. He kissed her. I saw him kiss her.

This should not be done. If someone other than I had found out… this could be horrible for her. It could be horrible for everyone. What on earth is she thinking?

My dear Heavenly Father, I didn't want it to be true, but I confirmed suspicions today with this one act.

I pray for guidance.

Standing outside the barn, Alston found himself shivering. This time of year, shaking like this only came because of anger or fear. Calm by nature, he wasn't accustomed to losing control. His emotions overflowed from him so fast that he wasn't able to stop the movement in his legs. He felt like a caged animal pacing back and forth in a cage of his own making.

"How could you be so careless?" he whispered.

Looking around the farm, Alston made sure that they were alone at the abandoned barn. They weren't far enough off the road to give them the protection that he desperately wanted at that moment. If someone was to wander by they would be able to see people at the barn. In a small town like Everett Springs, someone would stop to help thinking that there may have been automobile trouble. Even worse, they could alert the local volunteer fire department fearing a fire in the dry field or barn.

Alston had to grab Eliza's attention and get her out of the area before someone saw her. A discovery like this could have disastrous consequences. Weighing his options, Alston realized that he could do only one thing in the short amount of time available. He had to confront his sister.

He took several deep breaths to slow his heart rate as he walked around the side of the barn. In his nervousness, the brittle, parched grass under his feet sounded as loud as the crackle of thunder in a storm. The walk took mere seconds yet felt like hours. Alston reached the barn door before he was able to fully prepare for what would happen next.

Steadying his breathing in an attempt to gain control, Alston lowered his eyes and whispered a simple prayer.

"Dear Heavenly Father, please prepare my heart so that the words from my mouth match the wish and desire you have for this situation. May your will be done. In Jesus' precious name, Amen."

Alston placed a flat palm on the weathered barn door and began to slide it open. The heavy wood creaked with the sudden movement. The barn groaned as he struggled with its rusty hinges, startling Eliza and her young friend. Alston moved the door enough to squeeze through. At the same time, they pushed through the heavy door at the opposite end of the barn and began running toward the empty field.

"Wait!" shouted Alston. "Stop, Eliza. Now!"

Hearing a familiar voice, Eliza stopped cold. She began begging the person she was with to keep going. Alston saw a teenaged boy standing in the middle of the field looking back at his sister, his face twisted in fear. He stood motionless as if he were deciding if he should run to save her or run to safety himself.

"Run, Eldridge! Go! Don't stop!" screamed Eliza. "I'm fine. Go, on!"

Eliza struggled to close the barn door creating a barrier between her brother and her companion. As soon as Eldridge was out of site, Eliza burst into tears. Covering her face as she dropped to her knees, she grabbed her brother's legs and began begging him to stop the pursuit.

"Please, don't go after him, Allie. Look at me. Stay here and talk with me. Please let him go!" Her tears fell as she began crying audibly and continued to beg. "Look at me, Allie. Look at me!"

Distraught, Eliza's body finally gave way and acted against her. Alston saw her form crumple onto the dirt floor of the barn. She didn't have the power or energy to do anything but weep. Her cries grew louder as she kept repeating, "Just look at me, Allie. Not him, just me."

Alston stood there, stunned. His mind raced from thought to thought. He was angry that his sister had kept such a dangerous secret from him. Fear held him captive.

Alston knelt and wrapped his arms around his sister, hugging the sobbing teenager. He moved her hands away from her face and held them in the palm of his own. The damage that these kids could cause to both their families made Alston want to lash out at her. At the same time, Eliza was his baby sister. She held such a special place in his heart that he could do nothing but place his arms gently around her to console her.

"Oh, Eliza. What were you thinking? You can't do things like this in Everett Springs."

His sister's tears continued to fall as she gasped for breath between quiet wails.

"Let's stand up. Look at you. You've gotten dirt all over your beautiful skirt. Mama will not be happy if that stains. You look just like Bette Davis, remember. Sweetheart, we've got to get you up before you do more damage." As angry as he was, Eliza was his sister, and his heart broke with every tear that fell from her big green eyes. He wanted to protect her, not make her cry.

Alston had a war of conflicting emotions welling up inside of him.

"Please, Allie, you can't tell Mama you found me here. I don't know what Daddy would do to him," Eliza begged.

"Daddy is the last of your concerns. Do you realize what could happen to you had any number of men in the county caught either you? You shouldn't have been here. Who was that boy? Tell me. You have to, Eliza, and now. I demand it."

Alston wasn't used to being firm with his sister. Under the circumstances it was easy as long as he ignored her tears and focused on the terror that held him hostage.

As soon as she was standing, Eliza threw herself into Alston's arms, crying and pouring out her soul to her best friend. She told her older brother about the love she had for the boy who she had met walking home from town one afternoon.

"Eliza, you can't be serious. A white girl and a colored boy isn't just against the law, baby. It's dangerous."

"But he loves me, Allie," said Eliza.

Alston rubbed his forehead and tried to think of a way to make his sister understand. "I'm not just concerned for you. It's me and Anne, Mama and Daddy, even Eldridge and his family. You're too young to understand."

"No, I'm not. I understand what life should be like. The only thing I don't understand is what it is. Eldridge should have been standing here meeting my big brother instead of running home. He shouldn't be worried about an angry wood shop teacher chasing him through a field. That's what's wrong. Please, Allie, you have to keep my secret." Eliza stopped sobbing long enough to look up at her brother.

"Eliza, I just don't know if I can."

CHAPTER EIGHT

The drama in the journal continued to unfold before Lizzie. Within the covers of the tiny, worn leather diary the details of the relationship played out. In her mind, she heard the arguments between Alston and Eliza. Lizzie could feel the fear that gripped her great-grandfather when his sister admitted that she was in love with a man of color. Even Lizzie knew that it wasn't a safe choice for a white girl living in the Deep South during the 1930s. Polite society didn't discuss Jim Crow's south, but Lizzie knew that it wasn't acceptable. She could picture the heated exchanges that the James family must have had around their kitchen tables then.

Lizzie read until her eyelids felt as heavy as lead. Jack's snoring jolted her out of the diary's grip. Leaning forward to see her antique two-belled alarm clock, Lizzie realized that the morning was coming fast. A little sleep was necessary if she was going to make it through lunch with her grandmother.

"It looks like I'll have to meet you in the morning, Gramps." She closed the diary and placed it next to her on the bedside table.

As Lizzie slept, she tossed and turned while the journal's scenes played through her dreams like a movie on a theater screen. Not knowing what Eliza or Eldridge looked like, she allowed her imagination to fill in the details. The familiar faces of Hollywood began acting out the roles of each character in the story. Eliza appeared on the dirty barn floor in her flowing skirt. In Lizzie's dreams, her great-aunt looked just like a cross between a graceful Ginger Rogers and a muddy, potato-wielding Scarlet O'Hara.

Lizzie woke earlier than normal with a million questions buzzing through her thoughts. Taking a pen and paper from the nightstand drawer, she began to capture her questions in ink before they flew out of her mind.

Sounds from the floor below caught her attention. Lizzie could hear her husband moving around the kitchen. She could picture Jack filling his thermos with hot, black coffee as he packed his lunch for a shift at the station. She loved that he got ready for work every morning in the same, methodical order. His consistent behavior made her feel safe.

Lizzie tossed the pad of paper onto the bed and flung back the heavy quilts. She wanted to make sure she spent time with him before work, filling him in on the diary's latest twist of events. She headed straight for their cramped walk-in closet for her favorite slippers and robe. Old farm houses had drafts that required a good pair of slippers in the fall. Luckily, Lizzie's obsession with warmth and comfort meant she was always prepared. Lizzie crossed the bedroom until she caught a glimpse of herself in the standing mirror in the corner. Giggling, she broke into an impromptu twirl. With her jade green robe and ruby red slippers, she felt like a character from The Wizard of Oz.

"If only I had my Toto."

As Lizzie entered the kitchen, she saw that Jack had poured her a fresh cup of coffee. Next to her steaming cup was a toasted bagel and her favorite light vegetable cream cheese.

"Once again, you prove to me just why I keep you around." Lizzie walked up behind Jack as he washed his breakfast dishes in the sink. She pressed her face into his back and wrapped her arms around him, hugging him like she hadn't seen him in days.

"Don't you forget it," replied Jack. Wiping mounds of soap bubbles from his hands, he swiveled in her arms and pulled her in close. "So, give me the skinny on what Gramps had to say. I woke up at two a.m., and you still had the light on. How late did you stay up reading, anyway?"

"I wasn't up much after that. It is so interesting, Jack. I think I'm beginning to understand Eliza's secrets."

"Do tell…" Jack laced his arms across his chest and leaned back against the kitchen sink. "Secrets, huh? Sounds juicy."

"My great-aunt Eliza was in a relationship with an African American man. Well, if you want to call a seventeen-year-old boy a man." Lizzie crossed the kitchen and sat down at the table to enjoy her coffee and bagel as they talked.

"That's not exactly the big secret that I thought it was going to be. Two teenagers dating. Really risky. Well, unless Daddy had a shot gun and little Eliza was home late after a date," teased Jack with wink. He refilled his mug with strong, black coffee and joined Lizzie at the table. Jack checked the time on the time-worn pocket watch that he carried just as his grandfather had. Leaning back to prop his feet onto the seat across from him, he added, "I've got a little time for a few more details."

"You've got to put it into perspective. This was happening in 1934. I don't think that was a normal occurrence then at all. Remember, Jim Crow laws were in effect up until the 1960s. We are talking about a time when they weren't even allowed to go to the same school much less date. I mean, this was risky business. I've got a ton of questions for Gran today."

"What did your great-grandfather write about it? I bet he flipped his lid."

"I don't know how it ended. I'm not that far into the diary yet. Alston seemed scared in the entries that I read. I spent a few hours going through them, but there's so much more in those pages. He spent a lot of time begging her to keep herself safe. Several times he wrote that he asked her to stop seeing this boy so that she wouldn't bring attention to herself or to their family." Lizzie took another bite of her bagel. "I didn't get the feeling that it offended him as much as you'd think back then. I think he was more afraid."

"Afraid of what? Their parents?"

"I guess. I read a handful of entries that made it seem like Alston and my great-grandmother, Anne, discussed it at length. They even had Eliza out for the weekend so that they could talk to her. I guess it was a Depression-era version of an intervention. He wrote like it was a pretty big deal. I think they tried to handle it quietly. He seemed pretty close with his sister."

"Did Big Brother get his way?"

"It doesn't seem like it. Eliza seemed to be pretty convinced that she was in love. Can you imagine that? At fifteen or sixteen years old? She was so young."

"Doesn't sound that crazy to me. I knew that I was in love when I was sixteen." Jack stood up and put his hand on the side of Lizzie's face giving her a gentle kiss. Crossing the worn wooden floor, he placed his used mug in the sink and started gathering his case files to take back to the station. "If Alston was talking about shame in the first entry, he couldn't have been too pleased that she wasn't listening to him."

"Like I said, it seems like he was reacting out of fear or some sense of social responsibility. I can't get a bead on him. I'm not sure if he was scared for her or himself. I know he was concerned that others not find out. He hasn't been crass about Eldridge being black, which surprised me for the period." Lizzie paused. "That's his name. Eldridge."

"Eliza and Eldridge. So, Gramps used his name. That has to give you a hint about it. He didn't call him something else at least."

"Who knows? I'd think if he were an out and out racist I would have heard the 'n-word' by now." Lizzie took another bite of her bagel and wiped her mouth with a cotton napkin. "I think I might do a little research today. I want to see what it was like back then. I just don't know where to start. How on earth do I find out what it was like to date outside your race then?"

"Google is your friend, my dear. It knows all." Jack picked up his keys and slung the strap of his messenger bag over his shoulder. "Let me know if you find out anything good. You're meeting Miss Gertrude this afternoon, right? Why don't we meet up in town for a beer and a sandwich after your visit with her? I'll treat. We'll call it date night." He leaned over to place a kiss on the top of the head and then walked towards the door.

"Sounds good. Meet you at Gill's? Six o'clock? I'll be meeting Gran for lunch, and then I'll just go hang out at her house for a while. Maybe she's got something else hidden in that attic of hers that would be neat to look through. I mean, she kept the diary from me for all these years. You never know what else she'll have up there."

Jack walked out the screened door toward his truck. Just as the door bounced against its wooden frame she heard her husband call out, "Call me at the station if you find a body up there."

Lizzie crossed her arms and leaned against the back of her chair. She noticed the sun shining brightly through the white kitchen curtains, and Lizzie couldn't help smilng. Her grandmother had finally won. After years of begging her to take an interest in her family's history, curiosity had finally gotten hold of her.

***

After a quick shower, Lizzie slipped into a comfy pair of boot-cut jeans and a blue and green knitted sweater with a cowl neckline. Although she was able to dress casually at work, it was nice to wear what she wanted rather than what fit a dress code. Her naturally curly hair just needed a quick towel dry and some gel to keep it in check. Since it was a day off, she skipped the makeup but layered on her favorite necklaces and bangle bracelets. Buckling a leather wrap belt around her waist she stood in front of the full length mirror. This time her reflection showed something more like her and less like a Munchkin from Oz.

"Better," Lizzie giggled.

Heading downstairs, she grabbed her laptop and settled into her favorite chair in the corner of the sun room. The large cushions were a little less firm than when she purchased the chair a decade ago, and the flowered print had started to fade. Even with its wear, it was still her favorite piece of furniture in the house. The sun room was her favorite place to sit when she had the house to herself. The morning sun streamed through the white eyelet curtains and flooded the room with the brightest light that she had seen in a long time. The grandfather clock in the corner chimed. She had two hours until she needed to meet her grandmother in the park for lunch. It was just enough time to research what life was like for an interracial couple in the 1930s.

Lizzie drank the last of her coffee and started searching the Internet. "Let's see what you've got for me, Google," she whispered.

History had always been one of her favorite subjects in high school. She couldn't remember the subject of interracial relationships showing up in her American History class. She had no idea what she would find. As she clicked links for blog posts and history journals, she realized that the past was darker than she thought.

After clicking a series of links, Lizzie discovered a local college's history department website. "Bingo!" she yelled. Besides documenting a complete list of race-based Jim Crow laws, the website included a time line showing changes in the social history of Georgia. Lizzie ran a finger down the laptop screen looking for entries related to the 1930s.

Lizzie's stomach sank as she read an entry related to miscegenation that included a definition.

"Miscegenation: the interbreeding of people from two different racial backgrounds."

"You've got to be kidding me," she said into the empty room. She continued reading.

"Starting in colonial times, laws preventing interracial marriages and relationships, or miscegenation, were common across the United States. Once considered something only found in the American South, these laws can be found across

the country. They remained in effect in various states until 1967 when the United States Supreme Court ruled them unconstitutional in Loving v. Virginia…"

Halfway down the web page, Lizzie found a link titled, Miscegenation Laws in Georgia. She scanned the list until she found the laws during Eliza's life.

1926: Colored clergy can marry Negroes only. Other marriages are to be nullified.

1927: White persons may only marry other white persons. All persons with ascertainable traces of Negro blood must marry Negroes only. Penalties include up to two years' incarceration.

1928: Miscegenation is declared a felony.

Lizzie picked up the diary and looked for the date of the first entry. On the top of the second page she located it: 1934. Looking back to her laptop, she scanned the list for that year's entry.

1935: It is illegal for a white person to marry anyone other than another white person. Felony conviction requires one to two years imprisonment for both the male and female as well as the performing clergy.

Lizzie needed a break. She sat the laptop on the ottoman in front of her and walked into the kitchen for another cup of coffee. Her mind raced with the implications of Eliza's relationship with Eldridge. From what the college website said, the relationship would be illegal not only in the state of Georgia but also in other states as well. She couldn't comprehend living a life during a time where she had to consider the law over her heart. Reaching into the fridge for her carton of vanilla creamer, Lizzie's eyes landed on a photo of her and Jack. It was a candid shot of the two laughing together when they were in high school. She couldn't remember who took the photo, but she did remember her feelings that she had for Jack that day. It was the same feeling that she imagined Eliza having when she looked at Eldridge.

Returning to the sun room, Lizzie continued researching the life that her great-aunt would have lived. At the bottom of the web page below the time line, she saw a link titled, "Interviews and Articles." Faces of young and old sat on the screen before her. Below each photograph were dates and notations that gave hints to their experiences.

Jailed.
Hanged.
Lynched.

As Lizzie read through the social history of the times, she read personal accounts that tied her stomach into knots. Originally she thought that her great grand-father was just concerned about what the neighbors around town may have thought about his sister's relationship. Now she realized that Eliza's relationship with Eldridge wasn't that simple. It wasn't just illegal. It could have led to a lynching or a murder.

After an hour of research, Lizzie was exhausted. Flipping through the pages of the diary, she once again read the words of her great-grandfather after she discovered his sister's relationship. This time, the emotions weren't foreign to her. Lizzie found herself worried about Eliza just as Alston did.

"Oh, Gramps. No wonder you were so afraid for your sister."

CHAPTER NINE

On the way to the park, Lizzie stopped by Gertrude's favorite bakery for chicken salad on freshly made croissants. As she walked through town, Lizzie patted her bag to reassure herself that the diary was safe and sound. Within minutes she could see her favorite park come into view. As soon as she crossed the road, she noticed her grandmother sitting on the park bench underneath Lizzie's favorite tree. Sitting next to Gertrude were Blue, Abi, and Claud.

"Gran, I only brought two sandwiches. You should have told me we were having a party!"

"Oh, we brought our own, dear. In fact, we brought enough for everyone," Claud said as she patted her picnic basket. "We've got finger sandwiches and crudites. There's a little meat and cheese. I also packed a few small salads. Bread?" Claud held out a bag filled with soft rolls made earlier that morning.

"Miss Claud, you're fantastic. I think we'd all starve if we didn't have you, and I truly mean that." Lizzie gave her a huge squeeze around the neck. "Have I told you how much I love you lately?"

"Oh, Lizzie, dear. You're just a peach. I'm just sharing what I love with the people that I love most. We should move over to the picnic table and start eating before the ham gets cold."

"You'd think she was feeding an army," Blue chuckled. "We're thankful, Claud, but our thighs aren't going to be tomorrow."

The ladies gathered their bags and made their way to the picnic table near the side garden. It gave them a perfect view of the park with all the color of the fall flowers and trees. Just beyond it sat the gazebo and roses. Lizzie stood by the table looking across the landscape. Even though she had visited the park only a day before, there was something different about it. She always felt grounded in this space, but today she felt more connected. Maybe it wasn't the park. Perhaps it was her. She took a deep breath of the clean fall air, and placed her meager lunch offerings in the middle of the pile.

Gertrude smiled as she opened Lizzie's purchase. "You brought my favorite sandwiches. Thank you dear. It's wonderful," she said as she placed a squeeze around her granddaughter's shoulders. Lizzie noticed how happy her grandmother looked that afternoon. She wondered if she was feeling that same lightness that Lizzie did. It didn't make sense how one evening together could have made a difference, yet somehow it had. She walked over to the table and took a seat between Abi and Blue.

"So," Blue interjected, "how far did you read in the diary last night?" Always ready to cut to the chase, she got the group focused on the task at hand. "Visiting with you old fogies is nice, but I want to hear that we successfully hooked the kid with the diary."

"Oh, you definitely did that," said Lizzie. "I read through at least ten or fifteen entries last night. I had a hard time not moving forward too quickly. I understand why you said to take it one at a time. Sometimes I had to read the entries twice just to keep some of the details straight in my mind. The emotions were so easy to get lost in."

"That is definitely true, dear. It was a difficult journey for you, I suspect," added Abi. "Where did you stop?"

"Alston had just found the Eliza and Eldridge in the barn. His sister was falling apart in his arms. I'm so tempted to ditch the lot of you so that I can catch up on the story!" Lizzie smiled and leaned to bump shoulders with Blue.

"I was a little surprised that you didn't call me this morning to discuss it. I wondered for a little while if you weren't as interested as I thought," said Gertrude.

"That's definitely not the case. In fact, I don't want to hear any comments from the peanut gallery, but I actually did a little research this morning online to find out what it may have been like for Eliza and her friend."

Each lady sitting at the table let out a gasp of surprise.

"I knew it! We got her!" yelled Blue as a curled hand shot in the air proclaiming victory. The group of friends broke into laughter as she wiggled and danced in her seat to carry the point home.

"It was just a little bit of research, so don't get too excited. I was curious and needed some history to put it into perspective. I couldn't tell if Alston was angry at his sister or scared for her. I needed to find out what could have scared him." Lizzie looked down at her plate and played with her napkin. "I have a tough question for you, Gran."

"Tough questions bring tough answers, but I'm ready," said Gertrude.

"What was your family's idea of race, Gran? I know how you raised me, but how did your father raise you? How did his father raise him?"

"You're asking if they were racist. Just call it like it is," said Blue as she dabbed the corner of her mouth with a napkin.

"Well, dear, it was a different time. Keep in mind that life wasn't like today. This was before the Civil Rights Movement. Jim Crow laws were still in effect down here. We had separate lunch counters and swimming beaches when I was growing up. We weren't allowed to go to school with each other, so it wasn't like we were encouraged to be friends. However, your great-grandparents wouldn't let me get away with using derogatory terms like I wouldn't you. My daddy was friends with the janitor who was a colored man. That's the word we used then. Colored."

"It was considered a polite word choice. Can you believe it?" asked Abi.

Claud nodded and said, "Looking back it wasn't polite at all, but it was better than the alternatives."

"Were you allowed to have friends of color then, Gran?" Lizzie reached across the table for the bottle of lemonade.

"Well, yes and no. Like I said, we weren't in school together. I lived in town because my parents wanted to raise me away from the farm. Location alone meant that I didn't have many children around me that weren't, well," she paused. "There weren't many children around my home that weren't white."

"Don't try to be safe and quiet about it, Gertrude," spoke Blue. "It wasn't a nice period in time. You can't make a silk purse out of a sow's ear." She rolled her eyes and muttered under her breath. "Just tell it like it is without all this sugar. You can't make it sound pretty no matter how hard you try."

"You're right, Blue. I know you're right." She took a deep breath and smoothed the top of her pants with her hands, composing herself before moving on. "In that case, no, I wasn't allowed to make friends with children who weren't white. I want you to understand the whole picture though. My father wouldn't allow me to do anything rude or impolite to anyone, period. He had a favorite saying: 'Everyone has a name.' That was his motivation for everything. If my parents found me to be mean or naughty to someone, he would ask me for the person's name. It was an immediate reminder for me to realize this was a human being that I was speaking to or about. I had to recognize their worth. Do you understand?"

"I'm beginning to, I think," said Lizzie, though she was not sure that she did.

"Look at the lesson. Only things in this world of value have names, you see. It was a very subtle way for my father to remind me to see the value in that person. It was also a way to keep me from using the terms that others used in that time. Those words were not tolerated in my home. I believe that he was trying to make better choices for me in that way."

Abi patted Gertrude's hand. "Your grandmother wanted to befriend everyone. It didn't matter to her one way or another which way God colored them before He placed them on this ground."

Gertrude smiled at her friend. "When I was about six or so, I met a little girl that lived down the road from my grandfather's farm. She and I were about the same age, or from what I can remember. My Daddy grabbed me up and brought me inside. He never said that I couldn't play with her, but he didn't take me back to the farm for a while. When I was older I just assumed it was because we were different. Your great-grandfather was a quiet man when it came to this area, so it wasn't something we talked about." Gertrude fought against the tears that were welling up in her eyes. "When your father was growing up, I thought that I was going to be different. I wasn't going to let some silly rule stop him from playing with any child he wanted. My father and I never had words over it, but I think I held a chip on my shoulder against him for it."

"You never asked him about it?"

"No, but after reading his diary I believe the way that he brought me up was a direct response to what he experienced with Eliza. I just didn't understand it then." Gertrude dabbed her eyes with her napkin before placing it onto her plate.

"He did seem terribly afraid in his diary. Why was that?" asked Lizzie.

"It was such an ugly time, Lizzie." whispered Claud. "Such an ugly time. I was still living in Florida then. Remember I grew up there. It just felt so dark and ugly when you'd see people like the KKK holding rallies and parades. The hatred was out in the open for all to see. Such ugliness."

Claud's words trailed off getting softer as she finished speaking. Her eyes looked across the park as her memories took her back to a past time. Lizzie realized that each women sitting at the picnic table had her own stories to tell. She wondered how many were filled with fear like Alston's.

Lizzie hesitated before speaking. "Did we have family in the KKK, Gran?"

"To my knowledge, we did not. I know of a few boys from high school that were in the Klan. We always knew about it but couldn't come to terms with why they did it. It didn't seem like their nature. Do you remember that?" Gertrude looked toward Abi and Blue for input.

"There was the Cranston boy," said Abi. She placed her sandwich back on her plate and wiped her mouth. After taking a sip of lemonade she continued. "He was in it, but I suspect that it was under duress. Remember, he got out of town as quick as he could and away from that mean daddy of his. I think he joined the service, didn't he?"

"Yep. Lost him in Korea," Blue confirmed.

"We also had Billy Conrad. You remember him, don't you? He was sweet on our Blue," added Abi again with a smile.

"Well, why wouldn't he be?" Blue smoothed her hair with her right hand while her left hand landed on her hip for a little wiggle. "I am beautiful after all."

"Humble, too. Don't forget that," snickered Gertrude.

Lizzie noticed a change come across Blue's face. She could feel the mood of the group change as the laughter quieted. Her happy friend became solemn in a way that Lizzie had never seen before.

"Billy Conrad was one of the sweetest boys that I knew," Blue said. "We lost him to his daddy." She quietly sat down and lowered her eyes as if to pray. As Blue's emotions changed so did that of the others.

Gertrude interrupted her friend. "Lizzie, dear, what Blue means is that Billy took his own life. It was such a great shock to us all," she said as she lowered her eyes. "His daddy had taken him to a lynching, and the boy just couldn't handle what he saw."

The word hit Lizzie in the heart. *Lynching.* The stories she read earlier that day came flooding back into her mind. She could picture the images on the college website. Broken and beaten bodies flooded her mind. She didn't know what to say. She was horrified at the experience that was so closely connected to her family while feeling heartbroken for Blue at the same time.

"His daddy was responsible," Blue said with anger. "I will never agree that Billy did anything to harm himself or take his life. The boy was too young. That man caused it. That man caused Billy's death. He should have been held responsible."

Lizzie couldn't remember the last time that she saw Blue angry or upset. Her grumpiness was typically reserved for those who irritated her in small ways such as the bag boy at the Piggly Wiggly who couldn't remember to put her eggs in a separate bag. Lizzie had never seen Blue show pain like this. She got up from the bench and stood behind Blue. She wasn't sure how to mend the hurt, but Lizzie couldn't stop herself from trying. As her head fell on Blue's shoulder, she whispered, "I love you."

Blue dotted her eyes with the white handkerchief edged with a delicate flower motif that she always carried in her purse. She patted Lizzie's arm and gave her a squeeze back as best she could from the awkward angle. Without her normal wit, the aged woman seemed more like a young, sad girl who could only nod and return a hug without words. The years may have passed, but the hurt that Blue felt was still written on her face.

"I didn't realize that this was something that affected everyone on such a personal level," said Lizzie. "I only thought about how it affected Eliza's life. I didn't realize we'd be digging up scars for y'all, too."

"We all have scars, dear. You couldn't grow up during that time and not get burned a little. Just like today, the world had a lot of evil in it when we were growing up. I pray God has a lot of mercy because people definitely don't have it for each other." Abi spoke with such sadness in her eyes that Lizzie could feel that somewhere under her aged exterior she had a story as well.

"Gran, is that what your father worried about? Was he scared of the KKK?" Lizzie was shocked that she was asking the question. Two days before, the idea that her family could be involved in a situation with the KKK seemed so foreign to her. She sat stiff in her seat, preparing herself for her grandmother's answer.

"With that we've gotten to where we all knew the conversation was going to end up eventually," sighed Abi.

"I'm so sorry, Miss Abi. I didn't mean to ruin everyone's mood," Lizzie said.

"Dear, you had to ask the question. We knew it was coming," Abi replied.

Taking another slow breath, Gertrude answered the question. "Yes. He was afraid of them. My father writes more in depth about it later in the diary, so I don't want to ruin the story for you. You are on the right path, unfortunately." Gertrude walked over to where Lizzie was sitting with Blue. "I think you're getting ahead of yourself. You said the last thing you learned about in the diary was that he confronted his sister, right? You've got quite a ways to go before you get into some of the heavier topics."

"There are heavier topics?" Lizzie said with an uncomfortable laugh.

"Oh child, just you wait," Blue said, having recovered from the earlier memories of Billy Conrad.

Lizzie grinned, happy to see her friend back to herself. "I want to know more about your grandparents. Do you know how they reacted to their daughter's relationship with Eldridge? The diary didn't seem to mention it."

"I'm not sure. Remember, I learned about it from the same place you did. The diary is all I have to draw on since Daddy didn't discuss it." Gertrude stood and began gathering up the leftovers from the meal.

"How do we find out more about it then?" Lizzie reached around her grandmother to gather the used plates and cups from the table.

"What did you do this morning when you needed more information?" asked Claud.

"I looked online." Lizzie saw the eyes of her friends light up. "No, I researched. I guess I'll just have to do a little more of that, now won't I?" Lizzie teased. She knew that the ladies were enjoying their time with her, and she was giving them the show that they wanted. "Don't you ladies get too excited, but if I wanted to do some real research beyond Google, would someone be able to help me?"

Laughter erupted around the table catching the attention of a group of young mothers pushing designer strollers around the walking path nearby. Lizzie couldn't tell if they were annoyed or entertained by the rag-tag group before them.

"Honey, you've come to the right place!" Abi grinned, thrilled to see that their plan was working. The diary had gotten Lizzie's attention just as planned.

Lizzie looked across the table. She was amazed at how the women in front of her worked together like a well-oiled machine, gathering odds and ends as they shared the details of their lives. She realized how much she missed them. These ladies were both friends and family to her. A quiet smile came over her face as she continued to watch how each played a role in the conversation.

The women sat together for a little longer, each telling tales of the past and teasing Lizzie about her new found interest. Lizzie hadn't been this happy in quite a while, and she suspected that the ladies felt the same way.

CHAPTER TEN

Memories of the past flooded Lizzie's mind as she walked up the stone steps of her grandmother's gray two-story house. She could picture Jack at the door for their first date and the photographer directing their movements during their wedding photos. She remembered the hours she and Gertrude spent hanging holiday decorations together. Rather than head home before meeting Jack for dinner, Lizzie spent the afternoon with her grandmother. She relished the chance to spend the afternoon asking questions about her grandfather. Gertrude welcomed the company.

The house wasn't large by today's standards, but it was large enough for those who lived there throughout the years. The porch stretched from the left wall of the home across to the right. Unlike Lizzie's farmhouse, Gertrude's porch extended only across the front. Since she was a little girl, the porch was always the perfect place for a deep conversation.

Lizzie leaned against a long pillar at the corner formed between the steps and the porch. She gazed up through the rafters and noticed each weathered board.

"Gran, do you ever think about moving out of this big house?"

"Not on your life. Your grandfather saved his money to provide this house for his family. I inherited it from him. Your father would have received it next, but one day it will be given to you. This place is going to stay in our family unless you decide otherwise. Its fate rests on your shoulders. Treat her right or I'll haunt you," her grandmother said with a devious smile.

Gertrude sat down on the porch swing that hung at the far right side of the porch. Patting the seat she said, "Come swing with me, dear."

Lizzie took her usual seat next to her grandmother. When she was a little girl, she spent hours sitting on this swing, rocking back and forth as she dreamed of her life as an adult. The chains holding the swing in place gave a familiar creak as her weight shifted into position next to her grandmother. The wood was smooth despite its age. The swing had withstood the elements well over the years. Granted, there was no snow to weigh it down or rot the wood. Rain didn't beat in past the overhanging porch roof unless a large storm came through. The swing stood strong and looked as if it were promising Lizzie that it would be here another twenty years.

"What was your father like, Gran?"

"Oh, my. He was a fine gentleman. You would have liked him, and he would have liked you. He loved to work with his hands. You know that he was a woodworker, right? He taught Wood Shop at the high school. See that railing? He made that and carved the detail by hand. I remember the summer that he put it in. This porch didn't have side rails like that when I was little. My mother just knew that I was going to fall off and crack my head wide open, so she made my father put one in. My father didn't do anything half way. He took all summer carving the designs around each spindle. It made my mother crazy! She just wanted a simple railing so her daughter wouldn't fall. Daddy knew it would be more important than that. He knew that townspeople would be walking by seeing his work on their way to church or school. It led to other jobs around town as people made changes to their homes. He had foresight. He also made it for you, dear."

"No, he didn't, Gran!"

"Yes, he did. He knew that if it was properly made it would be here for future generations like you."

"I'm glad that he made the time to make it beautiful then. He was quite talented," Lizzie said. "You should be proud."

Gertrude smiled at her granddaughter. "He was a quiet fellow, but he loved to talk with family and friends. He just wasn't the loudest in the bunch. He liked to keep a low profile."

"Do you think that influenced how he handled the situation with Eliza and her boyfriend?"

"Most likely. He wasn't one to bring attention to himself. His woodworking was different. In real life, he liked it quiet." Gertrude paused. "He loved her deeply, you know. As a big brother he felt responsible for every bad choice that she made. Her victories were her own to celebrate, but he felt that her failures were in part his responsibility."

"What happened to Eliza?" Lizzie was impatient to know the full story. Learning the story in small increments was excruciating. She wanted to rush to the answer so she could understand more about her great-grandfather. She began to feel uneasy when she considered how much about her family she didn't know. As of now, there was a large void of answers. She was desperate to find out what happened.

"You'll learn more as you keep reading the diary. I can't tell you yet. It's like the end of a movie. You just have to get there for yourself or I'll ruin it." Gertrude stood from the swing. "I forgot to tell you that I looked through some boxes last night after I talked with you on the phone. I found something that I think you'll like."

Gertrude and Lizzie wiped their feet on the rough welcome mat and walked through the front door. Typical for its period, the home's front door opened into a wide foyer and hallway. Rooms placed on each side of the hall transitioned from the more formal in the front of the building to the informal kitchen in the back. The first room to the left of the foyer was the sitting room. Lizzie noticed a stack of photo albums sitting on the end of the coffee table near the front sofa. The thinnest album in the collection lay open in the center of the table.

"Did you bring those down by yourself? You're going to hurt yourself one of these days."

"It was worth it. I found a photo of Eliza, and I wanted you to see it."

Gertrude lifted the photo from an old black paper album littered with crooked photos that had tattered edges. She held it out to Lizzie for her to examine. Lizzie's heart skipped a beat. She glanced down to see three beautiful young women standing with arms linked on a red dirt country road. Farm land stretched behind them with fields of cotton dotting the landscape. The girls looked no more than fifteen years old. Lizzie knew immediately which one was Eliza. It was like looking into a mirror. It could have been a high school photo of Lizzie staring back at her.

"Gran, is that Eliza in the middle?"

"Good eye, my dear!" Gertrude was thrilled that Lizzie noticed the resemblance as well. "She was beautiful, wasn't she?" Her voice trailed off as she stared lovingly at the photograph.

Lizzie never considered her own face to be beautiful. She would believe pretty, but not beautiful. Seeing Eliza in this way brought a new perspective. There was no arguing Eliza's beauty. Lizzie shared her same dark hair that fell gently around the curves of her face. She had the same piercing eyes that caught the attention of those looking at her. The old photograph made Eliza's skin tone look like porcelain. She seemed so happy. Lizzie could imagine the laughter shared between the girls as they stood linked arm in arm like partners in crime. Eliza's head leaned so that it rested on the shoulder of the taller girl to her left.

"Who are these two," Lizzie asked as she pointed to the other girls in the photograph.

"I'm not positive, but they remind me of my aunts on my mother's side. I suppose that they could be her friends. Either way, this photo shows a happy young lady without a care in the world. Doesn't it? This would have been right around the time my father's diary entries began. She had such innocence here. I'm glad the camera captured how happy she was."

"What do you know about your Aunt Eliza? Who she was and what she was like?"

"She was a beautiful soul. My father talked about her like she hung the moon." Gertrude placed the photograph back into the album. As she talked, she flipped pages gently pausing to let her fingertips run lightly over the faces in other photographs. "She was the youngest of his siblings. As the oldest he was often in charge of looking after her when her parents were either in the fields or otherwise engaged. They were extremely close. I think that had she lived, Eliza would have been a constant figure in my life. Her loss greatly affected her family."

"You said that the diary talks about what happened to her, or how her life ended."

Gertrude reached over to hug Lizzie around the shoulders. "You're so impatient, my dear. We'll talk about it when you get to that point. Until then, let's look at some photos."

Lizzie sat on the floor like she had as a child, searching through album after album. As her grandmother shared family stories, Lizzie saw faces and personalities emerge. Lives that she didn't know existed became three dimensional. Bit by bit, Lizzie learned the stories that connected the generations in her family tree. Names grew into full and complex individuals as she learned that some had children while others struggled. Mothers held fast to their children as their husbands fought in the military and made history through war after war. Finances were destroyed when The Great Depression landed in Everett Springs. Vivid stories of horrific events spelled disaster for relatives that she hadn't known existed. Throughout each story, Lizzie began to see a theme develop. Each person learned to move through tragedy to become stronger. As one photo album closed another would open.

Reaching into the pile for a new album, Lizzie grabbed one bound in red leather. "Hey, this is one of Mama's old albums." She smoothed her hands over the embossed *H* that sat in the middle of the front cover. Lizzie opened the album and turned to the first page. In the center of the page was the last family photo Lizzie had taken with her parents. The photograph was perfect. Her mother's smile glowed. Rather than looking ahead, her father turned his face to look upon his family with adoration.

Lizzie found herself thinking about that night. The accident wasn't her father's fault, but it didn't matter. Lizzie's father was driving them home from a church event when the weather shifted without warning. A normal Wednesday evening turned into her worst nightmare. The storm started off as a gentle rain.

Within a few minutes, the winds were heavy and the thunder crashed like the sound of dynamite exploding overhead. Hail began to pound against the car like gunfire. Lightning flashed like fireballs. At twelve years old, Lizzie thought she was brave but that storm scared her more than anything had before in her short life.

As Lizzie started thinking about the storm, the emotions of that night came rushing back. She could still hear her mother's screams erupt from the seat in front of her. Looking through her grandmother into the past, her eyes saw her dad try to gain control of the car. All Lizzie could do from the backseat was hold onto the door handle and pray. She felt helpless, and in a few short minutes she would be helpless, too. She could feel the vinyl under her as the seatbelt tightened her against the back of the seat. The car spun around and around the small, two-lane road in slow motion.

Lizzie raised her hand to touch the scar on her forehead where she hit the glass window. Then, her memories of that night went black. Lizzie had no memory of what happened next. She only remembered waking up in the hospital with Gertrude sitting next to her singing Amazing Grace. Only Lizzie had survived the crash. From that moment on, Lizzie lived with the loss of her parents and the pain of final memories. Lizzie carried the weight of the accident with her daily. If she hadn't begged her parents to stay for the children's ministry event at church, Elton and Grace Hines would be alive.

The room around her spun back into focus. Lizzie could hear her grandmother talking to her about the family photo that Lizzie now held in her hand.

"So, you see, dear, there is adversity in each generation," Gertrude said. "We all need to remember that. Our ancestors fought through hard times to build a stronger life. You are a fighter, too. Learn from their lives."

"I'm learning, Gran. I promise."

After a good time together, Lizzie left to meet her husband for dinner. Hugging her grandmother, she promised to call in the morning to discuss the next batch of diary entries that she read.

As Lizzie walked down the series of steps that led from Gertrude's house to the street, she turned to look over her shoulder. "I love you, Gran. You know that, right?"

"Yes I do, my girl. And I, you. Don't you forget it."

CHAPTER ELEVEN

Looking at her husband across the bar table, Lizzie couldn't help but smile. She was thankful that she had him as a friend and mate. People began filling the local establishment, and as they did many stopped by the table to say hello to the County Sheriff's Deputy and his wife. The restaurant was the Clydells' version of a place where "everybody knows your name." They enjoyed the relaxed atmosphere and how easy it was to just unwind for a few hours over an appetizer and a cold drink.

After dinner, the couple decided to take a walk through downtown. The night air was cool and crisp but still warm enough to enjoy a walk after dark.

"There won't be many nights left like this," Lizzie whispered as she hung onto Jack's arm. The downtown area of Everett Springs had seen a revival of late. New stores opened next to pharmacies and shoe stores that had existed for generations. The mix of old and new brought a cozy feel to the town.

"Spending time with Miss Gertrude like this is good for you," Jack confided in her.

Lizzie stopped in front of the dress shop window. Everything looked perfect in a shop window. Each piece was in perfect position, displayed without confusion, emotion, or drama. She caught her reflection in the glass. After a draining day of family revelations and memories, she felt far from the perfection she saw before her.

"Why does everyone keep saying that? It's getting old, Jack. I'm spending some time with the gals and learning a little family history along the way. That's all. You don't have to fix me, and if you did, this isn't how I'd suggest going about it."

"You have had a lot of pain and baggage that you haven't dealt with over the years. You think that you've healed. You haven't. You've let it define you instead. Learning about your family's struggles and how they shook off problems might help." Jack took Lizzie's hand in his and continued down the sidewalk.

Lizzie didn't want to admit that her husband was right. Still, a few family stories weren't going to fix twenty years of pain and guilt. The situations were completely different. A new hobby wouldn't erase the baggage that she carried even if it was an enjoyable way to spend the fall.

"Let's head home," Jack said as he put his arm around his wife's shoulders. "I've got an early day, and you have a diary to read."

Although she had to work at the community center, the couple had decided that it was a good time for Lizzie to take a break. She rarely took time off, so her boss jumped at the chance to let Lizzie use her vacation time. A few weeks off to play detective digging in her family's past would be fun.

Once home, the couple started their new evening routine. As Jack ran on the treadmill, Lizzie pulled on comfortable pajamas and settled into bed with the diary. Flipping through the pages, she found the next entry and began reading.

***

Diary of Alston James: 26 August 1934

Eliza is distraught, and for once I don't know how to fix it. My concern for her continues to build as I learn more about her relationship with the colored boy. There is just too much danger. Not only do I worry about our family and even his, but I worry about others who might know. She doesn't understand the complexity of the situation. It's much too big for her to grasp at this age.

God created us to love. Scripture tells us that. But like this?

Mother suspects something. She can tell that her daughter is in love by how Eliza is acting. She is concerned that Eliza is too young, that I know. She wouldn't approve of any boy today, even if he was a white boy. I have yet to tell her or Father. I've promised to keep this between the two of us until I know what to do. I have to proceed with caution. I've begged her to stop seeing him, but she just won't listen.

I think she believes that she'll run away with him.

The spirit of the town is changing. Some are starting to rally. The klan is beginning to show up to events, and I have heard talk of it at school. I know the heart of everyone in the town isn't with them yet. Those damn hoods just make it so difficult to know who exists within the ranks. It's those few who make it difficult for the others.

One sinful, dark soul can pollute a mass of people.

We've got laws, but what laws will they look at? The laws of marriage in the courthouse or the laws of life and death? Will they come for her and take her to where they torture like that which occurs at the cemetery? I've heard the stories. I've seen the tree.

I have to protect her. I can't allow her to come to danger. It isn't allowed because they won't allow it. She is only one small girl.

I must pray. I have to pray.

Alston walked along the stone path toward the church. It seemed like the most natural place to be after he came to the realization that he couldn't discover the answer without prayer. Walking into the church he immediately felt better. The weight of the situation somehow lessened. Alston hoped that he could find solace in the pews.

He made his way to the second row of seating on the right side of the church where his family always sat on Sunday mornings. Alston's father feared that if they allowed the children to sit farther back they would entertain distraction.

"Children need to focus on the message," he said.

The church was the one place away from home where Alston felt at ease. At the high school, he had to hold himself stiff and present the face of a man older and wiser than he felt. He needed to act mature in order to receive respect. Around town, he had to show that he was an educated city dweller not the farm boy who got teased in high school for being dirty. At home, he had to be the provider for Anne and the head of the household. Things were different at church. He could be himself.

As he leaned against the wooden pew, Alston noticed the church's stained glass windows. Each window displayed an ornate design. Considering the age of the church, it was much grander than most would expect. The congregation had a remarkable appreciation for sharing God's word. Several large endowments allowed them to install the beautiful stained glass windows. Each section depicted Bible stories that the congregation felt were important. It reminded him of days told through history when churches used art to explain scripture to the illiterate.

Alston's favorite was the window depicting the Parable of the Prodigal Son. The beautiful slices of colored glass outlined the three men in the story. The father was full of love and forgiveness, looking upon his sons. The two younger men stood in contrast to each other. One son was dutiful while the other was not. As Alston looked upon the glass, he couldn't stop wondering if perhaps Eliza was the prodigal sister. He began to see himself in the glass as well. He felt like the other brother, dutiful and determined to protect his father's possessions. In the parable, the younger son had returned. He allowed his mind to dream that one day she would be returned to dutiful behavior like that son.

He opened his Bible to Luke chapter fifteen. Reading the passage, Alston's conscience jolted him. He had to forgive just as the father had forgiven his son. Like that very son who threw himself into his father's arms, Eliza had thrown herself into his at the barn. Over their times of conversations since, she had asked for his forgiveness and love. Alston had no other choice.

He lowered his head and began to pray.

"Dear Father, who loves us like no other. I thank you for the opportunity to bring to you my burdens and those of my sister. Please, direct me in how I should bring peace to the situation. Please protect her as she doesn't understand the gravity of what she's done with this boy. I pray that I will be a vehicle of peace and forgiveness, yet also one of repentance. Please help me protect her. If the community should find out her secret… Protect Eliza and Eldridge through this ordeal, Lord, for I fear that they need it."

Alston raised his head to look again at the colorful stained glass windows that held stories of forgiveness and love. He couldn't help but feel anger toward his sister for the danger she was putting him in. Even as he prayed, he fought tears of shame, anger, and frustration. Looking at the panels of stained glass to his left, he felt immediately convicted. Alston saw a message that answered his prayer immediately. It was a stained glass depiction of Jesus writing a name in the sand. Alston knew the parable. Jesus had been protecting a prostitute from a stoning that the crowd believed she deserved.

"Those without sin shall cast the first stone," Alston whispered. Placing his hands in his pockets he bowed for one final prayer. "I am not without sin, Father. I will not cast a stone. I just pray that you give me the provisions to protect them and their secret."

Preoccupied with his own troubles, he didn't notice that there was a young boy sitting in the pew alone in the pew behind him. Looking around the sanctuary, Alston saw the child's father speaking with the pastor. The child sat swinging his feet back and forth with the quiet look of boredom on his face. It appeared that the boy was looking at the same stained glass windows that had held Alston's attention just moments before.

"You like that window, son?" Alston asked as he turned toward the door.

"I do. That man looks happy," replied the little boy, pointing to the father in the Prodigal Son window pane.

"It's a story of forgiveness and love. The daddy in that story loves his son and forgives him. We need to remember that we need to forgive the trespasses of others when they repent. I needed the reminder today. Did you?"

"I guess. What's a trespass?" he replied.

Alston winked at the child and tousled his hair. "See you on Sunday," he said as he walked out of the church sanctuary.

The boy's father walked toward him from the rear of the church. After a heated argument with the pastor, his temper had remained. As the man walked over to the pew that held his son, he waved his hand and growled, "Git. Let's go."

"Daddy? Why would somebody pray about a secret?" asked his son as he ran to keep up with his angry father.

"Why do you need to know? You got one?"

"No, sir. I don't keep no secrets. I swear. But Mr. Alston there said that Eliza and that nigger boy Eldridge had a secret. He was praying about it. Why would he need to do that?"

His father stopped short causing the boy to bump into his father's legs. The man turned to look at his son. A new flash of anger streaked across the rough, cold eyes of Greer Abernathy. His hands tightened into stiff fists by his side as he tried to hold back the anger.

"I don't know, Thomas, but I can tell you that I mean to find out."

CHAPTER TWELVE

Lizzie squinted at her alarm clock after several hours of fitful sleep. Reading her great-grandfather's diary left her dreaming of his fears instead of resting.

"Four a.m. I guess I'm not sleeping tonight."

She eased out of bed trying not to wake Jack as he snored. As she tip-toed downstairs to the kitchen, the only sounds she heard were the creaks of the old farmhouse. She grabbed the tea kettle from the stove and began filling it at the sink. Lizzie looked out the kitchen window across the back field of their property. Her barn was newer in construction, but in her mind's eye it became the old, run-down barn where Eliza and Eldridge met. She turned on the stove to heat the water for tea and dragged a quilt to her reading chair. After filling her cup with a heaping scoop of loose tea and hot water, she settled in to read more of her great-grandfather's diary.

Lizzie snuggled underneath the quilt and took a sip of tea. Jack's photo on the mantle caught her attention. She had fallen in love with her husband around the same age that Eliza had fallen in love with Eldridge.

Lizzie felt another deep connection to the woman who was her namesake. Thumbing through the diary to find her last entry, Lizzie began thinking of herself as Eliza.

The next few entries in the diary were a quick jumble of emotion. Alston's entries held little detail of the events of Eliza's life. Instead of giving Lizzie insight they only created more questions. Shorter entries followed, and Lizzie's eyes grew heavy. Before she knew it, Jack was waking her up with a kiss as he left the house for work.

Lizzie wasn't used to being alone in the house for long periods of time. Thanks to her impromptu vacation, there was nowhere she had to go. The day could be anything that she'd like. Picking up her hands-free Bluetooth ear piece, she called her grandmother while she cleaned the kitchen.

Gertrude answered the phone on the first ring. "Good morning, darlin'! Did you sleep well?"

"As a matter of fact I did not. It's all your fault for getting me hooked on this diary." Lizzie giggled as she said it. "That father of yours left me confused once again. There was such detail and emotion in some of the entries, but then a few left me with more questions than answers. It was like an emotional roller coaster so I tossed and turned all night."

"Did you read about the church?"

"I did. I had no idea that the window we sat next to each Sunday had a connection to our family." Lizzie slipped her hands into the sudsy water to wash the morning breakfast dishes. "We have a lot of history in that church."

"You've had it on all sides. Your people on the Hines side were founders in the town, but you knew that. They were in the pews from the beginning of the church as well. My family was, too. I believe your mama's people went back several generations as well. Remember, she used to work in the ladies' garden. Your mama was so talented with those roses."

Lizzie stopped washing dishes for a moment. She began to smile at the thought of that many generations in her family together. She could picture them sitting together in the pews; laughing, crying, and singing through services. She was also surprised at how relaxed and comforted she felt confronting a memory of her parents. Normally she would be bristling at the reminder of all the moments she would miss without her mother in her life. The change surprised her.

Gertrude's voice brought her back to the present. "Tell me, where are you in the time line? What did you read last?"

"Eliza was missing, or so your dad thought. Do you know what happened during that time?"

"Daddy found her. You're just about to get the details." Gertrude hesitated. "You should read it for yourself. Why don't we meet up for some research later? I'm meeting the gals at the library later. Are you in?"

"Sounds good to me. I'll drive. See you in an hour."

After finishing in the kitchen, Lizzie tossed her clothes in the dryer and showered. It sounded like she was going on an adventure with her grandmother. While she waited for her jeans to dry, she sat down on the bed with the diary.

She didn't expect what she was about to read.

***

<u>Diary of Alston James: 2 September 1934</u>

Eliza is still missing. A few people in town saw her talking with Greer Abernathy. I'm not sure what may have led to that encounter, but I don't trust that it was a pleasant one if Greer is involved. Our neighbor saw him coming back from the cemetery with his sons just a few hours ago. He suggested I take a walk that way. Anne is begging me to wait until her brother can accompany me.

My anxiety may not allow me to wait. My journal holds my attention, but not for long.

I pray that I can bring my sister home safely and give me the insight that I need to handle the situation delicately.

Please, Lord, protect my Eliza.

Alston couldn't wait any longer.

"Allie, he'll be here shortly. Please, don't go alone," Anne begged.

"I have to find her, Anne."

Alston ran out the back door of his house to a path that cut through the woods. It wound through thick groves of trees and ended at the top of a hill that faced the cemetery. From the hill, he could see the entire area including the cemetery within its iron gates and the river that ran alongside it. Just beyond the river sat a field that hadn't been farmed in generations. The geography created the perfect location for those wanting privacy. It was also known as a meeting location for organizations like the Ku Klux Klan.

Though most men Alston knew in town wanted nothing to do with the Klan, a few caved to the pressure of family or employer. His loose association with them allowed him to be privy to whispers of names. Rumors surrounded the involvement of the Abernathy family. If there were, Alston doubted it was because someone forced Greer into participation. His stomach tied in knots at the thought that Eliza could be in the cemetery. If Greer was there, it would be a dangerous situation.

Alston ducked under tree limbs as the path opened up to the cemetery. He hurried to look for signs telling him if his sister was there. As he ran past the trees he came to the crest of the hill. Alston's heart sank as he reached the gates to the cemetery. Panicked, he looked everywhere for his sister. Tied to the iron gate was a length of frayed white cloth. Alston's blood ran cold. Even though he wasn't a member, he knew what it meant. There had been a meeting of the KKK.

"Eliza!" he shouted. "Where are you?"

Alston saw a short length of rope flicking in the wind from behind an oak tree off in the distance. Alston ran to the tree. As he came near he saw a broken body swinging from the rope that looped over the largest branch. Blood streamed down the man's face where he had been beaten. His eyes were swollen and his was skin torn in deep, wide cuts. Even with the damage, Alston recognized immediately that the man was just a boy. It was Eldridge.

Alston ran to Eldridge, grabbing him by the legs. He struggled and slipped in the dirt and mud as he tried to lift the boy to relieve the pressure from the noose. His body was too heavy. Alston tried to wrestle his body free but realized that the rope would have to be cut down from the top. He tried to reach Eldridge's neck to feel for a pulse. The boy's arms rattled by his sides as Alston pulled and tugged at his limp body.

Alston ran his hands over the pockets of his jacket and pants looking for his knife. Struggling up the tree, he wriggled and climbed until he was able to reach out far enough to the rope that wound around in knots. Sawing back and forth, Alston ripped each fiber in an attempt to set the boy free. The fraying rope popped, dropping Eldridge's limp form to the ground. Alston watched his legs fold under him as the last thread in the rope snapped. He jumped down to the ground, landing on his knees. He rushed to Eldridge feeling for a pulse or breath. Instead, the boy lay broken and lifeless.

Alston sat back onto his heels and cried. He dragged Eldridge into his lap by the straps of his overalls, dirty and stained with blood and red clay. Weeping, he looked at the boy's body. His right ear was missing, and his arms were broken. Eldridge's shirt and overalls were ripped and fraying along the back. Ropes hung from his wrists.

With his arms still wrapped around the dead boy, Alston leaned to the side and was sick. He knew immediately that the poor boy was dragged to the tree. Broken hearted, Alston tried to wipe the blood off the head of the boy to whom his sister had given her heart.

As his own tears poured out, Alston heard the cries of another. Crouched behind a headstone several rows away, he saw another broken and battered body. His anger boiled when he realized that this wasn't the body of another young man.

It was Eliza.

Alston ran to his sister, pulling at her arms she had raised to hide her face. He was shocked at her appearance. Her hair had been ripped from the neat bun she had worn earlier in the day. Blood stained her clothing. Alston grabbed at her body, turning her from side to side checking her for injuries.

"Eliza, let me see," he yelled as she fought against his hands. "It's me. Allie. You're safe with me now. Look at me, Eliza."

Alston brushed the hair away from her face to find the same bloody wounds and swollen eyes that he had seen on Eldridge. A large gash cut across her face extending from below her left ear to her right cheekbone. She fought him, slapping his hands as he examined her wounds.

"Leave me alone! Please, leave me alone," she cried.

Alston lifted her weak body into his arms. "I'm here. Allie has you. Can you talk to me? I'm taking you home, Eliza. I have to get you home."

Alone in the cemetery, Alston knew he had to make a difficult choice. He could only carry one of them at a time. He had to save his sister.

Alston looked over at Eldridge's lifeless body lying on the ground behind him. He said a quiet prayer and promised his sister that he would come back for him soon. He whispered to his sister, "Hold on, baby girl. I'm taking you home."

He stood looking around the cemetery for hidden dangers when he saw the road at the bottom of the hill. Knowing that he couldn't carry Eliza through the overgrowth of the woods, Alston ran down the hill toward town. His arms and back ached, but his fear kept him going. Soon he reached the town square, running alongside the open doors of businesses as people stared from inside. Horrified faces shaded their eyes and shied away from him.

"Help, please. It's my sister. She needs help!"

Women scurried their children indoors, and several men stood in the doorways with their backs facing Alston. No one came to his aid. With no reason to stop, he continued running until he reached his home.

Alston stumbled up the porch steps and banged on the front door with his shoulder, refusing to set Eliza down on the porch. Unable to open the door with her in his arms he began crying out for his wife.

"Anne, it's me. Open the door. Hurry!"

Seconds later, Anne opened the door with a gasp and cry. Her hand flew to cover her mouth. "Oh, sweet Lord, be near."

Only then did Alston start weeping over the broken body of his sister, Eliza.

CHAPTER THIRTEEN

Lizzie sat holding the diary in shock. They killed Eldridge? What did they do to Eliza?

"Holy crap," she said to the empty room.

A wave of emotion flooded over her. She didn't expect to grieve a life she didn't know. Lizzie couldn't believe how close she had become to the people represented by the words on the pages in front of her. She hadn't known that Eldridge existed more than a few days, yet she felt like she lost a family member. Her sadness flowed into anger. Lizzie resisted the urge to throw the diary across the room. She wanted to distance herself from it and go back to her blissful state of ignorance. Reading the next entry wasn't something she wanted to do. Lizzie had to see her grandmother.

Rather than waiting for her jeans to finish drying, Lizzie threw on yesterday's pair and ran down the stairs. After grabbing her keys and jacket, she flew through the kitchen door and ran toward her truck.

"The diary," she whispered.

Doubling back, she ran to her bedroom to retrieve the book. She had to get to her grandmother's as fast as possible. Lizzie needed answers, and she needed answers immediately.

As Lizzie's vehicle barreled down the gravel drive, she couldn't control her anger. Her knuckles began to turn white from gripping the steering wheel with all the strength she could muster. She slammed on the brakes and threw the engine into park, dust flying all around her. Lizzie threw the door open and jumped out, her boots sliding in the rocks. She couldn't sit still just yet. Adrenaline flowed through her body making her flush. She had to move. She had to pace. Lizzie moved back and forth franticly like an animal in a cage. Her shock over what they did to Eldridge turned into an anger that she hadn't felt since after her parents' accident.

Lizzie threw her head back and screamed to the sky, cursing God. "How could you do it again? Why do you keep taking people away from those that love them?"

She screamed at the passing clouds, tears running down her face. The wind whipped around her, blowing her hair into her face, causing heavy strands to stick to her wet cheeks. Her hands clawed at the chunks of curls, pulling them back and willing them to leave her alone. Pacing, she walked further down the drive. Without giving herself a second to think, Lizzie started kicking the closest fence post. Lizzie kicked the post with her boot, over and over, until the red dirt around the post's foundation stained her boots and jeans. Dust swirled around her, hanging in the air like a tornado.

"Why did they have to murder Eldridge?" she screamed. She threw her head back and yelled till her lungs burned and her throat as on fire. "What the hell did you let them do to Eliza? Why do you always have to take everyone?"

Lizzie's legs trembled, struggling to hold her own weight. She grabbed the post in front of her to steady her body until finally giving in to the weakness. She slid down into the gap where the driveway's rocks met the red clay and grass in the side ditch. Lying on her back with her knees bent in the air, Lizzie clutched her stomach and gave into the tears that wouldn't stop. She cried over the loss that she felt for Eliza and Eldridge. Lizzie couldn't explain the hole she felt growing inside her. The feelings were overwhelming until she realized that she wasn't just crying for them. She was also crying for the others missing from her life. Lizzie was crying for her parents.

After laying by the road for what felt like hours, Lizzie stood. She dusted the dirt off of her clothes and piled her hair into a loose bun using the elastic that she always kept around her wrist. She climbed into the truck and sat behind the wheel. Void of all tears and emotions for a few moments, she pushed the engine into drive and continued to Gertrude's. She pulled out onto the road in front of her farm and turned toward town.

By the time Lizzie was in front of her childhood home, she was ready to discover the details that darkened her family's history. Lizzie tilted the rear view mirror toward her and wiped her eyes for one last time.

She looked at herself in the mirror and paused. "Let's do this." Lizzie walked up the stairs to her grandmother's front door. She stood for a moment, took a breath, and knocked.

Gertrude opened the door, surprised to see her granddaughter. "Lizzie, oh my stars! Are you all right? Sweetheart, what's the matter?" She wrapped her arms around Lizzie's shoulders and pulled her into the house.

Her grandmother set Lizzie in the sitting room and retreated to the kitchen to make a tray of tea and fruit. Lizzie looked around the room filled with antiques and family heirlooms. Lizzie and Gertrude sat together in heavy silence, each stirring their own cups of tea.

"Is this how the house looked when you were growing up?" she asked her grandmother.

"Well, yes, I suppose. It was similar. Of course I've added a few things over the years. I don't live in a museum. Things change." She took a sip of tea. "Why?"

"After reading about Eliza today, I can't help but think of what it looked like that night. I just walked up the stairs that Alston carried Eliza up. This is the house where he brought in a battered and bruised sister to recover. It happened here, Gran. Not somewhere unknown. Here. He brought her to the house where we live."

Lizzie's composure started to break as she began telling her grandmother what she had read. The strange mixture of anger and sadness flooded her again. Tears began to roll down her cheek.

"I just can't believe what I'm reading. You learn about events like this, like the lynchings, but you don't think you've got them in your family. This was all because two kids fell in love." Lizzie took a slow, long sip of her tea and sighed. "Gran, I thought I was just reading about two star-crossed lovers. I was hoping Eliza and Eldridge would run off to New York where she could be a writer. Jack has been pushing me to finish my degree. I thought you were giving me a story of love and determination. I was so wrong."

Gertrude patted Lizzie's knee and gave her a smile. "Oh, baby girl. I thought you knew it wouldn't end well. It was a different time. They weren't supposed to be together as far as society believed at that point. They were taking a risk in trying to be together, and they knew that." She reached for a box of chocolates that she kept on the side table for guests. She held the open box to her granddaughter. "Chocolate is the best medicine."

"Where were they for those two days? Held? Trapped?" Lizzie sat with the chocolate in her hand, unable to focus on anything but the story.

Gertrude stood and walked to the front window. She swept the lace curtain from the window and placed a hand on the glass. She stood quiet, watching the neighbor children as they played between their yard and hers. "My father indicated in his diary that they had been missing for a day or two before the incident. I think that they were trying to run away together just like you thought. Where else could they have been? He didn't write that she was held captive, so they had to be together before that mob found them. I don't think they expected what happened."

"Do you know what happened to Eliza?" Lizzie hesitated. She wasn't sure she wanted to know the answer to that question.

"You know from the diary entry that they beat her pretty severely. Just like Eldridge, Eliza's wrists had the same rope tied around them. My guess is that they dragged her just as they dragged him, but I don't know that for sure. Daddy believed that they raped her. You'll read about it later in the diary. During her recovery Eliza kept telling him that the men involved told her that she needed to be 'turned back to her kind'." Gertrude lifted a handkerchief from her pocket and patted her eyes as they watered. "The hatred that they heaped on that poor girl was too much. Remember, she was just a teenager herself. It was just too much."

"Gran, do you think if she had made a different decision they would be still be alive? If she had stayed away from Eldridge, would it have made a difference?"

"I wouldn't know how to guess. There's no way to know. All I know is what happened that day, or at least what the diary tells us," Gertrude answered.

"Do you know who did it? Do you think that it was someone in the town here today?"

Her grandmother was silent. "I'm not sure that I want to know that answer. Do you?"

"I don't know. Don't you think that it's time we found out the full story? Eliza deserves to be remembered. We have to find out what happened to her."

***

After a light dinner, Lizzie sat in the glider in front of a fire. She looked up at the first stars of the night and made a wish.

"Wish I may, wish I might, have this wish that I wish tonight. I wish that Eliza's story will be discovered."

"Did you say something?" Jack asked as he joined her in the back yard.

"Oh, just being silly. I'm making my wish like we did when we were kids. Who knows? Maybe it will work this time."

"What are you wishing for? I know. You want a handsome man to come sweep you off your feet." Jack pulled his wife's feet into his lap and pulled off her boots. "Tell me your story."

Lizzie had been replaying the diary entries in her head all evening. Like Technicolor film, the horror her grandfather expressed in his diary played on a loop through her mind. She replayed the details from the diary as well as the fear and anger she felt as she broke down in the drive.

Jack sat in the dark listening. Finally he asked, "Are you sure you need to go through this? Maybe the diary is too much for you to read. It sounds like it is just ripping off a scab from a wound that healed a long time ago. If you keep chasing this thing you'll be stirring it up for everyone in town. Is that what you want? We're talking about confronting racism in the South, Lizzie. This is beating a hornet's nest."

"But, Jack, don't you see?" Lizzie pleaded. "This is about a life that the people of this town swept under the rug. We're talking about a murder, Jack. What if they are running around town here today?"

"I think you've lost your mind. They'd be at least 100 years old by now."

"There was a mob, Jack. Some of those boys could have been teenagers. There are people in this town that are that age. They could still be alive. There could be other entries in the diary with more details leading to the people who murdered Eldridge. That's a crime. You investigate crime. What about the crime involving Eliza? We're talking murder and rape, Jack. You can't let that go."

"Now I know you've lost your mind. You can't be serious. It's an old diary, Liz. Listen to how it's written. It's not exactly filled with specific names and locations."

Lizzie decided right away that Jack had no idea what she was holding. This diary was the story of a relationship gone wrong. It was the story of a family torn apart. She couldn't be just the keeper of these secrets. She had to do something about it.

"I don't care what you think. These lives need to be remembered. They need us to find out the truth. You're supposed to find justice for the innocent victims. Listen to what my great-grandfather writes. His heart was filled with so much pain. His sister and this man were victims. Don't you believe that the stories in his diary are true?" Lizzie sighed under breath. Jack hated it when she sighed. In her heart she hoped that this would land with the impact she intended. "Jack, this is for my family."

"I love you and your family, but we're talking about an event in history that people don't want to discuss. I think you need to put this into perspective. Remember their lives, but don't look for a crime. Do what you need to do to make peace. There's nothing more to do than that."

Lizzie didn't appreciate the brush off that she received from her husband. She knew that Eliza and Eldridge needed to be remembered no matter what Jack said. It was time to hit up Gertrude and the gals for help. Her mind raced with questions. Where should she look? Newspapers? The courthouse? An event this big that ended in the death of one and the rape of another had to be recorded somewhere. "Gran and the gals will know," she whispered to herself. She leaned back into the glider and looked at the stars once more. "I'd like to be a little clearer on that wish of mine…"

Lizzie walked inside and got ready for bed. She pulled the covers around her body and settled in with the diary. Now that the initial shock had worn off, she had a renewed energy and interest in reading more. Lizzie read late into the night, even after Jack turned off his bedside lamp and settled into sleep. She couldn't sleep until she knew more about the pain that

Eliza felt. She had an empathy that she couldn't explain for the girl that she'd never know.

Lizzie couldn't stop searching until she had answers.

***

Diary of Alston James: 4 September 1934

My heart is so heavy.

Poor Eliza has been recovering for the last few days at my home. Anne is such a wonder to watch as she nurses the wounds of my baby sister, both those that are physically seen and those that are hidden emotionally. She shows such compassion that I pray her love and concern will nurture healing.

I'm not sure what Eliza remembers. She refuses to speak. She's locked herself into her mind, keeping us all out of reach. She withdraws whenever I get too close. She's so broken. My heart weeps.

I've been trying to contact the local police but no one wants to investigate a death like that of Eldridge. They won't investigate the crimes against Eliza. They say that it's illegal. They are so cruel and hurtful, looking past what they did because Eldridge was colored.

What about my sister?

I can see the light fading in her eyes. I'm not sure how long she'll be able to survive like this.

This is all my fault.

Alston paced back and forth in the second floor hallway in front of the closed bedroom door that held his battered and broken sister. Anne stood at the bottom of the stairs listening to him as he prayed and cried out to God. After hearing his footsteps slow, she made her way up the staircase hoping to find him in their bedroom ready to rest and relax.

"Allie, there isn't anything that we can do other than give her time. She might be ready to talk in the morning."

"We've been saying that for days, Anne. There's nothing I can do about what happened, but I can make sure that she doesn't feel alone. She was all alone out there, don't you understand that? I found her all alone in that cemetery with his body. They left her there like an animal." Alston walked into the bedroom and sat on the edge of the bed. Leaning forward, he held his head in his hands and the tears flowed. It may not have been a typical reaction for a man, he thought, but he couldn't hold it back. His life felt like it was falling apart.

"We should call the police again, Allie. They have to listen."

"They don't care. They won't do anything. There are too many people involved. We have to protect her. If she doesn't make waves, perhaps they will leave her alone. We just have to protect her and pray that they don't come back for her a second time."

Alston realized that he was the only thing standing between Eliza and those who attacked her. What if they decided to come after his sister again? What if they came after Anne? He reached toward his wife and held her face in his hand.

Anne laid her head in her husband's lap. "I keep thinking of the family that Eldridge left behind. It's so sad. Their hearts are breaking, and yet we can't grieve together."

"I can't get his face out of my mind. He was so young." Alston leaned over and buried his face in the side of his wife's head, feeling her hair cover his eyes. "I had to leave him, Anne. I had to. I had no other choice. I couldn't carry them both. I caused this."

"Alston James. Stop those thoughts. You did what you could, and you called his folks. Not many in this town would have done that. You didn't do it to him. All you could do was try to protect Eliza. No one will fault you for that."

Anne took a seat near her husband. She wound her arms around his as they sat at the end of the bed. The pair sat in silence. Alston wanted to become invisible and quiet. He had to protect his family, and if that meant becoming someone that no one noticed he would do it. He needed to do what would cause Eliza the least amount of distress and harm as she recovered. She had to be his first thought.

Anne leaned into his shoulder and started crying quiet tears. Alston cradled her into his arms as she emptied herself of the tears she had carried after days of tending to Eliza's wounds.

"We could leave, Allie. We could pack her up and go to South Carolina. I've got people there. You could find another position at a school, or we could farm. We could do anything. I just want to get out of this town, Allie. I want to be away from this place."

Alston looked at his wife's tearful eyes. Her bright blue eyes shined red and bloodshot. He brushed the hair from in front of her forehead and eyes as he wondered how long it had been since she had slept more than a few minutes. He knew that Anne was exhausted.

"Anne, we can't let them run us out of this town. I will keep you safe, and I will protect Eliza, even if it means keeping quiet."

CHAPTER FOURTEEN

After another long night with little sleep, Lizzie felt like she was stumbling through the morning. Her thoughts felt hazy and slow. The evening's discussion with Jack was heavy on her heart. He may have been right. Maybe there wasn't anything that she could do, but she wasn't going to let it go without trying. Murder was still murder. She had seen so many cases on the national news that centered on the same type of scenario: old crime gets solved and people go to jail.

After a quick stop by the local coffee shop, Lizzie met Gertrude and the gals at the local library. Her grandmother explained that it would be best to start with the local newspaper. Lizzie was anxious to see what they wrote about the incident. Gertrude warned her that they would most likely ignore Eldridge's lynching.

"It may need a bit of creative searching," her grandmother reminded her during their morning phone conversation. Lizzie was ready to spend as long as it took to find out the truth. Gertrude was willing to research as long as Lizzie wanted.

Lizzie met the four smiling women at the library, passing around cups of coffee for everyone.

"Nectar of the gods," slurred Blue as she drank the dark chocolate mocha she had requested.

They settled their belongings at the long table in the research room, each making sure the lid to her drink was secure and away from any of the library's materials. Claud made sure to point out the sign showing that they were allowed to have drinks at the tables only.

"Don't be so stuffy, dear. We know the rules," Blue said. "Of course, I never was fond of rules." She winked at Lizzie.

"It's time to introduce you to the microfilm readers. Be prepared to feel like you can't go any further. Once you get to that point, your record will be just around the corner," Abi said as she patted Lizzie around the shoulder. "Let the games begin!"

The women loved having Lizzie in their element. The foursome shuffled her through the library, showing her where to find the microfilm that might contain her records. Lizzie had no trouble narrowing down when the article may have been in the newspaper, thanks to the diary. Lizzie pulled three rolls of film from the metal cabinet covering the correct time period.

The women each pulled up a chair around the microfilm machine and began to show Lizzie the proper procedures in using the reader. Each genealogist had her own tips.

"Start at the beginning of the roll," one said.

"Read all of the entries for the week," said another.

They whizzed through the first roll showing Lizzie how to load and advance the film. The researchers turned the spools, slowly making their way through the old newspapers. Lizzie enjoyed the vintage ads and community reports listed on each roll. The information provided gave her an insight to the life her family lived during that time. It surprised her how interesting she found it all. Every so often, Lizzie would see a mention of her family name, usually the society pages that shared church rosters. The first two rolls didn't afford much insight into their mystery, but the final roll hit like pay dirt. The group of genealogists squealed when they located one mention of a potential event.

A newspaper article from the first week in September had a simple two word headline: *Negro Hanged*. The article detailed an event on August 30, 1934. Without flowery language or emotion it stated cold fact. An African American man approximately sixteen to twenty years of age was bound and hung over a tree near the old town cemetery just north of the town square. It provided no additional details.

"This is the cemetery that you're trying to save!" Lizzie cried out. Several annoyed researchers around her shushed in frustration. A woman near the end of the row of machines gave her a wink and a thumbs up for her discovery. "It happened in your cemetery?"

The lack of detail in the article shocked Lizzie. The article didn't mention Eldridge's name or the abuse that Eliza had sustained. The article reduced the cold, hard facts to a short line as if it were just another entry in the report of the town's comings and goings.

Mrs. Nash visits her sister, Mrs. Horn.

Everett Springs High School will be performing the spring musical this weekend.

Negro Hanged.

The reporter didn't glorify the event, but also didn't denounce it as a horrible act. It was as if they were reporting on the death of a farm animal. Lizzie kept reading through that week's edition for any mention of tragic events involving Eliza.

"There were no witnesses. The police have stated there will be no further investigation into the incident."

Lizzie leaned over to her grandmother who was scanning film at the next machine. "Gran, there wasn't an investigation? Are they serious?" she whispered. "I don't see anything about Aunt Eliza in here. Were her injuries just ignored?"

"Well, it was an unseemly and traumatic event. They didn't talk about rape in the newspapers like they do these days."

"Yet they'll talk about a lynching without calling it a murder. Those details weren't too gruesome, but these others are. Rape is unseemly. Lynching is not. Got it." Lizzie fought to tamp down her anger.

"Our family wasn't high society, but my father was a teacher at the local school and went to the local church.

The newspaper may have thought they were sparing them from a scandal. Eliza was having such a hard time dealing with it after it happened that the family could certainly have used the break. Maybe the newspaper had a little compassion."

"It just feels like they ignored her. This is hopeless."

Gertrude sighed. "I know it doesn't seem right. It isn't. Don't stop yet though, dear. One thing to realize about research like this is that you usually have to piece together many hints and clues. Rarely does your answer show up in one document. There may be another mention. We have to just keep looking."

"It's just so foreign to me. They mentioned it like a line item between the farm report and the classifieds." Lizzie rubbed her eyes with the palms of her hands. "I'm going to grab a drink. I'll be right back."

She needed to take a break. Sitting in the dark room looking at microfilm was stressful on her body and straining on her eyes. It was taking an emotional toll on Lizzie as well as a physical one. A small break would work wonders for her spirit and drive.

Lizzie had finished her coffee, so she walked out to the foyer of the library to the drink machines. She eyed the sugary choices in front of her and decided that plain bottled water would be best. The beautiful weather caught her attention as she walked past the library's picture window.

"Some sun will fix everything," she whispered.

Lizzie walked over to the small bank of benches that sat directly outside the library doors and took a seat. Stretching her legs out along the length of the bench,

Lizzie closed her eyes and leaned her head back. She took just a minute to let the heat of the sun wash over her. It felt marvelous, and a smile glided across her face. She did something that she hadn't done in a long time. She just breathed.

"How are you holding up, dear?"

Lizzie looked up to see Abi standing near her. Shading her eyes with her hand, she looked up at her dear friend. "I'm doing all right, Miss Abi. I just wish I'd find out more about Eliza and Eldridge. It's so frustrating not to see them get justice for what happened."

"That's the funny thing about family history research. Sometimes you find your story. Other times you simply find the mystery or, in this case, the horror. You'll get there. Keep searching. Your motives are honest and true. It will pay off."

"I hope so. I just feel like they deserve more. They deserve vindication or acknowledgement. Something." Lizzie sighed. "I guess we should be back at it."

"Let's get inside, then." Abi gave her a hug.

Lizzie turned toward the parking lot. "I'm going to grab my jacket from the car. It's a little chilly in the microfilm room."

"Hazard of the job, my dear," Abi said with a wave of her hand as she entered the library doors.

Lizzie stood and stretched her arms above her head. Putting her hands into pockets, she took off toward the car. Lizzie was surprised at how cool it was in the library. As she crossed the parking lot, she saw a familiar face.

"Well now, look who you run into when you come to town during the day!" Lizzie slid up behind Thomas Abernathy and put her arm around the elderly man's shoulders. "It's so nice to run into you."

"Miss Lizzie, look at you. I'm so glad to see you in town. Have I introduced you to my grandson, Avery?" Thomas gestured with a hand to the young man who accompanied him.

"It's nice to meet you, Avery," she said as she extended a hand. "I'm Lizzie. Your grandfather is a favorite of mine at our church. Are you in town for a visit?"

Avery Abernathy was a handsome man. In his early thirties, he was well dressed with a sparkling white smile. By the look of his clean khaki Dockers and his leather loafers, Lizzie could tell that he wasn't a man used to hard physical labor.

"Nice to meet you, Miss Lizzie," Avery said as he reached to return her handshake. "I'm here on a reconnaissance mission. I'm thinking of moving back to town. It would be nice to have family back in the area again, right Gramps?"

"It would be wonderful. I think you'd be quite happy here. Generations of your family have been after all. So, Lizzie, dear, how are the kids treating you at the community center? Are they here on a field trip today?" Thomas stood leaning on his familiar wooden cane. His smile lit up his face as he looked at Lizzie.

"It's just me today. I'm taking some vacation time this week to hang out with my Gran. We're digging into a little family history mystery. It's exciting."

"Gertrude has to be in heaven. You're making your granny very happy, young lady. Is this something you learned about when you were at the church the other day for the meeting?"

"Yes, sir. Did you happen to see the diary that was with us at the table? It turns out that it was my great-grandfather's. He used it to record his thoughts about an event that involved his younger sister, Eliza."

Lizzie didn't notice, but a look of concern flashed on Thomas' face. He made a quick inhalation which caught Avery's attention. Without losing composure, Thomas nodded and said, "Why, yes, I remember Miss Eliza. She was older than me, but I knew her from around church." He reached out a hand and patted Avery on the back. "Family is important, isn't it, son?"

"Yes, sir, it is. That it is." Avery followed his grandfather's lead but remained concerned that there was more to the story.

"I better get back inside. Gran and her friends are holding my seat at the microfilm reader. Those newspapers aren't going to search themselves," Lizzie giggled. She gave Thomas a friendly hug and turned to Avery. "Enjoy your visit here. Hopefully our paths will cross again. I'd love to introduce you to my husband, Jack. Maybe we'll see you at church on Sunday."

"Sounds like a plan. Nice to meet you, too." Avery gave her a glistening smile. As his new friend walked back into the library, he turned to his grandfather.

"So, Gramps, are you going to fill me in on what that was about? Who was Eliza?"

"She's the reason that I do what I do, son. She's why your mama left town. She's also the reason that I never could." Thomas wiped tears away from his eyes, hoping that his grandson wasn't able to discern the pain that he felt at hearing Eliza's name.

Confused, Avery patted his grandfather on the back. He looked in Lizzie's direction to be sure that they were alone.

"Why don't we grab lunch and talk for a minute," Avery said.

CHAPTER FIFTEEN

Thomas and his grandson entered the small diner and took a seat in a booth near the window. After ordering lunch, Avery leaned back into the banquet seat and looked at his grandfather. The older gentleman fiddled with the edge of the worn cloth napkin that sat folded by his coffee cup.

"Lizzie seemed nice," Avery said, starting the conversation with an easy topic.

"She is. I've watched her grow up. I've watched many in her family grow up. I guess that's what happens when you are one of the oldest in the church. You see generations grow up before you like weeds."

"You've know her family for a while then?"

"I've known both sides of Lizzie's family all my life. You heard me tell Lizzie that her great-aunt was someone I knew from church. You don't have to beat around the bush with me," Thomas said.

"You've got me," Avery said with a smile. "Who was she?"

"Eliza was the sweetest girl that I knew. She was older than I was, so it wasn't like we were friends. I guess I was a little sweet on her like all little boys are sweet on those older girls who take an interest in them." He continued to fiddle with the edge of his napkin until the hem curled in his fingers. The waitress brought their lunch and scurried off to take care of another customer.

"Are you okay to talk about this?" Avery asked.

"You need to know. It's part of your history." Thomas stirred a packet of sugar into his tea. "It never is sweet enough. Anyway, Eliza was a good girl. She would sometimes sneak me a piece of peppermint at Christmastime. I know that it had to be a sacrifice for her because her family was just a farming family like mine. We didn't have money for candy, and I know they didn't have much to spare either. She was special, that one. She died, Avery, and I caused it."

Avery set his fork down on the side of his plate. He wiped his mouth with his napkin and tried not to choke on his last bite of food. "I don't understand, Gramps. What did you do?"

"One day we were at the church. My father was mad at the pastor for something, so he had to go tell him about it. He had a violent temper, that man. I was just a young boy and had accompanied him there. I liked looking at the stained glass windows so I usually begged to go with either of my parents or older siblings when I had the chance. That day, I overheard a man praying for his sister. He said things that I was unable to understand. I was a child after all. After he left, my dad came out from speaking with Pastor. It was then that I made the most devastating mistake of my life."

Avery waited as his grandfather took a sip of tea. He could see his grandfather's hands shaking. "We don't have to talk about this if it is too much. We can wait until later."

"No, no. I'm fine. The truth has to come out," Thomas continued. "You see, I heard Eliza's brother talking in church, but I didn't understand what he was praying about. I was a young boy, so I did what young boys do. I asked my father. I didn't realize the implications, Avery. I didn't mean it." Thomas fought back tears. Setting his hands in his lap, he dropped his face and his voice. "My daddy made me tell him everything that I heard Alston say. All my father cared about was that the neighboring black boy was doing something that he shouldn't."

"What do you mean? What was he doing?"

"Eliza was going with him. I think that's what you call it today. She was sweet on him. It was a different time, Avery. Not like today. It wasn't allowed. I didn't understand what I had done until the next day when I saw him hitching up the horses. He told me that it was time for me to learn what it was to be a strong white man."

"Gramps, are you telling me that you were in the KKK?"

"No, not me, but my father was a member as was his father before him. I made a break from that life as soon as I could. I will not claim any alliance with such a group filled with hate. I've made mistakes in my life, but that isn't one of them. That damned organization caused me to become a player in a production that has destroyed one life after another."

Avery was speechless. He had learned about the KKK in school, but no one he knew had connections to an organization like the Klan. His world was simple and organized. It didn't have connections to a hate organization much less to crimes inflicted upon others. In a matter of minutes, Avery's world had become a place that was unfamiliar to him. It was a world that held connections to Grand Dragons and burning crosses just two generations away. He knew that his grandfather held the secrets of an elderly man, but he didn't expect to hear him disclose something like this. He looked into his grandfather's eyes and asked, "Then what happened?" unsure he wanted to know the actual answer.

Thomas pushed his plate away to the edge of the table. He waved the waitress over and had her remove the dishes before continuing his story.

"I learned what the word lynching meant," Thomas said just before breaking down in tears.

Avery was speechless. He covered his grandfather's intertwined hands with his own and said a silent prayer. He wasn't sure if he was praying more for his grandfather or himself.

"That night was the worst night of my life. I watched as your great-grandfather destroyed two lives." Thomas bowed his head and continued. "I was a coward hiding behind a tree that night. My father told me to stay put and not come out, but he made sure that I would be watching what he made my older brother and the others do to those poor kids. I saw more than I should have. He wanted to teach me a lesson, and he did. I learned to hate my father that night."

Thomas' eyes stared off in the distance. As he continued his story, his grandson realized that he wasn't just sharing a memory, he was reliving it.

"Tell me what happened, Gramps."

"Avery, I can still hear his voice…"

***

"Please, stop. You don't have to do this, sir. I'll do whatever you want. Just let the girl go," he begged.

A young girl's screams mixed with the shouts of an angry man in white as he gave orders to those around him. The hooves of the horses threw dust into the air around them as the two teenagers struggled. Bound by coarse rope at their hands and feet, they struggled to free themselves from their restraints. Cries and shrieks filled the air. Blood ran into the ground staining it red in a way that looked as if the entire earth was crying out in pain along with those in captivity.

A heavy boot landed on the ribs of the boy as he begged.

"Shut up, nigger. I said you needed to learn your place, boy. That's what got you into this mess. Not knowing your place." The screaming man yanked hard at the rope that connected his victim's hands, tying it to the back of the horse. "I'm teaching you now, nigger. Oh, I'm teaching you now."

The girl struggled to kick and scream. Three men in white repeated the process they used on the boy, connecting her by the same type of rope to a different horse. The hands of a teenage boy pulled at her dress a little too hard while he let his hands linger a little too long along her hip and thigh. She screamed and tried to roll to the side, kicking her legs while the tender threads of her dress began to pop and rip. Tears streamed down her face which was now dirty with red clay. Her gentle green eyes looked up at him as she pleaded for him to stop.

"Why are you doing this?" she cried. Her sobs fell as gentle as feathers yet landed like heavy boulders on her companion's heart. Looking up at his father, he seemed to be asking the same question.

His father saw hesitation in his older son's eyes. He threw down the rope that he was tying to the horse and walked over to the girl.

"You shut up, too, whore." He grabbed his teenage son by the straps of his overalls and shoved him toward her feet. "We don't talk to whores. Now get her tied, son. This is for her own good. It's for *our* own good. The girl needs taught a lesson."

Spitting a long, dark stream of tobacco juice out of the side of his mouth, his dirty smile grew. He knelt down next to the girl and began playing with the hem of her dress. He yanked and tugged at the fabric just to see her scream.

"Please sir, I'm beggin' ya," the bound boy pleaded. "I see what I did was wrong, sir. I did it. She wasn't willing, sir, I promise. I took advantage, sir," he screamed. "It was all my fault. Just take me, sir. She was a victim, sir. Please, Lord, spare her!"

The young man's soul seemed to scream out as he begged for the life of his companion. Instead of bringing her relief, his pleas only enraged the man in charge like gasoline on a fire.

"You want me to spare her? A whore? Y'all hear that? This nigger wants me to take care of a whore." Again he spit a long string of black liquid into the ground. Trails of blood and tobacco mixed into a vile concoction. "Come to think of it, my boy can do that. Son, come here. This girl needs took care of." He ran his fingers up her leg lifting her dress as he moved his hand higher and higher.

"But, Daddy, I don't want to…"

"Just do it," he screamed at the shaking boy as he shoved him to the ground on top of her.

The boy fell backwards into the dirt and struggled to raise himself. Panicking, he looked over at his younger brother as he hid behind a tree. He tried to rise up as the back of his father's hand landed square on his cheek.

"You will do as I tell you, boy. Don't you sass me," he yelled.

The man pulled out a heavy pocket knife and popped it open. The girl screamed as she heard the blade lock into place. In one fluid motion, he used the knife to disconnect the rope that tied her feet together. Immediately she started kicking both feet, aiming for any body part she could contact as she thrashed her body back and forth. Her screams grew louder and louder until her voice blended into one scream with the horses.

"Take him down to the tree," the man screamed. "Wait, no. He needs to watch. He loves her so much he wouldn't want to miss this." Motioning to another man, the leader had him dragged toward the girl while boots and bloody fists rained down upon him. The beating left him groggy, just alert enough to see the pain that the group was inflicting on the girl.

The girl's screams grew stronger and stronger until it appeared that she couldn't stand it any longer. Reaching her limit, she passed out. The mob swept over her, each taking a turn in violating the unconscious girl. One by one, the men began to move away from her, leaving her limp and unresponsive in the grass. As the dust began to settle, the only cries they heard were those from the boy lying in ropes next to her.

"Eliza!" he sobbed. "Oh, I'm sorry, Lord. I'm so sorry," he prayed just as another boot landed with a crack into the side of his ribs.

The man in white lifted him by the collar, bringing him upright so that he was able to see the damage they inflicted on the one he loved as she lay in the dirt next to him.

"See that, boy?" he said, shaking him with each word. "We didn't do that. You did. You're the one that hurt her, and you'll be the one that ruins her, too." He threw the boy back down into the dirt before slapping the hind quarters of both horses. The animals reared and then lunged forward, dragging the two teenagers up the hill.

Walking over to his son, the leader of the mob growled his directive. "He got to watch her suffer. Now it's her turn. Wake her up so she can see him swinging in the tree like the monkey that he is."

The blood-thirsty group of men mounted horses and followed the trail that led to the town's cemetery near the creek. The dust swirled around the bleeding and broken bodies for a quarter mile up the path and into the cemetery. The hate-filled war cry of the group created a roar like a monster heading for a hunt. Their victims bounced off of rocks and into trees that lined the path. The fabric on their bodies tore under the force of being dragged across the rocky dirt. Swelling had set into their faces so that they became unrecognizable. Rivers of blood poured down their arms as the rope began cutting into the delicate skin around their wrists.

As they arrived in the cemetery, the leader shouted orders to the men that he controlled, separating them into two. He ordered one group to deal with the boy while the other to dealt with the girl.

"Get her awake," he screamed with a flick of his hand toward the broken body of the young woman.

A man grabbed her by the arms and dragged her limp body to the creek that ran parallel where they stopped. With a handful of hair, he dunked her head down into the water again and again. She coughed as she revived. The cold, rushing water hit her skin, stealing what remaining breath she had. Once she was awake, he dragged her back to the scene sitting her against a tombstone just one row over from the tree.

"Here you go, whore. You got a front row seat for the show. We want you to be able to see everything, since you like looking at this nigger so much," one of them growled. He kicked her feet together and tied them at the ankles so that she couldn't run.

As she sobbed and begged for mercy, they hurried to drag the unconscious boy closer to the branch of the tree.

"Get him up there!" screamed the man in white. One group of men checked and tightened the ropes on command, binding his hands and feet tighter. Another group began to throw ropes around the boy's neck, creating a noose.

"Greer! You want us to wake this one up, too," another man asked.

"No, it's not worth our time," he replied. "Just get him up there. I'm done with this. We need to get done and clear out."

With quick movements and angry grunts, the team pulled the rope over the largest branch on the lynching tree. With great effort, the men began pulling and yanking the rope, till they had it secured to the saddle of the horse. The leader kicked the horse's sides. As the animal lurched forward, the rope slid over the tree like an evil pulley hoisting up the boy. Within seconds, his companion heard his neck snap as his body's weight pulled toward the ground.

The mob of men cheered as if it were a holiday while the young girl screamed out in pain. Her guttural sobs were the only thing that broke through the celebration. The men turned their attention to the girl, broken and slumped against the headstone. No one had noticed where they had placed her until that moment. Her limp form leaned against the tallest and most decorative marker in the cemetery.

Eliza was leaning against the headstone of a gentle man: the church's founding pastor. An angel carved of marble lay prone across a rectangular stone, weeping. Her wings lay limp at her sides draping over the edges as if to cradle the crying child on the ground below. The heavenly figure stood taller than those around her, forming a barrier between the girl and her attackers. Sculpted in the pose of mourning, her arms lay crossed under her head, obstructing portions of her face. Her body curved downward toward the broken form of the child she held close. The angel wept stone tears for the damaged girl below her.

The men grew quiet. Their celebratory cheering ceased.

All that they heard were the soft cries of a broken girl asking, "Why?"

***

The two men sat in silence. Avery propped his elbows on the table and lowered his chin against his clasped hands. His stomach churned after hearing the horrific details. He couldn't imagine living through them.

"It wasn't your fault." Avery said, trying to console his elderly grandfather. Thomas was an elderly man, but all Avery saw in front of him was a broken and hurting little boy.

"Don't you see, son," he said. "I wasn't the one holding the whip, but I was just as responsible. I never did leave that tree. I could have done something to stop him or to get help, but I didn't. My fear of my father was too great. Their blood is on my hands."

Thomas' eyes became glassy and his tone slowed to a more moderated, cold demeanor.

"Avery, my older brother was called by my father to punish the poor girl. He wasn't the only one, but he was the first. It ruined him. He may have died in World War II, but his heart and soul changed that day. My father didn't only destroy two teenagers that night. He destroyed three."

Thomas wiped his eyes with his napkin as he looked around to see if anyone else had heard his story. He reached across the table and grabbed his grandson's arms.

"When your mother heard this story, she decided that you weren't going to be raised in this county. She was afraid that people would learn the truth and that one day you would know what my father had done. I may not have a connection to the Klan anymore, but it is still around in the shadows. She never did trust me after she learned the truth."

His grandfather fell forward on the table whispering pleas to God for forgiveness. He begged for a second chance to make it right - one that he would never have as time wouldn't bend to his pleas no matter how hard he prayed.

"I've spent my life trying to make up for my sins by working at the church and giving back to Eliza's family in any way that I could. They've never known that it was me who told my father, but now with Lizzie looking into it who knows what will happen?" Thomas' voice trailed off. "What am I going to do if she finds out? I've loved that little lady since she was a tiny thing. She'd never forgive me. I just can't stand to see her look at me like your mama does."

Avery turned his head to look out the diner window. The glass was hazy from the steam coming out of the kitchen, but through the fog he could see a figure exiting the library. Lizzie Clydell walked across the parking lot to her vehicle.

"We'll make her understand if she finds out, Gramps. Don't you worry. I promise we'll be okay."

Looking at Lizzie, Avery hoped that it was a promise that he could keep for his grandfather.

CHAPTER SIXTEEN

Armed with her light jacket, Lizzie walked back into the library. The short break outside in the fresh air did wonders for Lizzie's determination.

"If Eldridge wasn't mentioned by name in the newspaper, what about Eliza?" she asked Gertrude as she sat back down at the microfilm reader. "Someone had to mention a local teenager who had died because of a violent encounter like this."

"Now you're thinking. If you hit a brick wall, look for another way around it." Gertrude smiled at her granddaughter. "Where would you start first?"

"You said to work backward in time, right? When did Aunt Eliza die?" Lizzie reached for her pencil and notepad.

"She died in October. My father wrote a short entry about it in his diary. I think it was the twelfth or thirteenth. Give one of those a try." Gertrude tilted her head back to look through her reading glasses as she continued to scroll through her film.

Lizzie pulled the diary from her bag. She thumbed through the pages until she found the correct entry. "Here it is," she said. "It was October twelfth."

***

Diary of Alston James: 12 October 1934

The Lord called home my sister today. The marble angel in the cemetery wept over her that night, and now they can rejoice in the calling home of another sweet soul.

I pray that my sister can finally be at peace. It wasn't something that she could get here on earth. I hope that she will find it in heaven.

My heart breaks for the loss of my best friend - my baby sister. How will I move through life without her?

I look into the eyes of my beloved Anne and wonder if I will be able to protect her any more than I could Eliza. The guilt I have is heavy. Oh, Lord, I failed her. I wasn't able to save her when she needed me.

Goodbye, Eliza. Your Allie loves you. You will never be forgotten as long as I have breath.

Alston closed his diary and placed it in the top desk drawer. Anne knocked on the office door just as the drawer clicked into place.

"Sweetheart, the funeral home has sent someone to collect Eliza. Do you feel like talking with them? Your father can't bring himself to do it. He needs you now, Alston, if you're able."

Alston walked his wife into the hallway. His father sat weeping in a chair in the front room, his hands covering his face. The sight caused Alston's chin to quiver. He placed a hand on his father's shoulder out of love and then coughed as he tried to stuff down his own emotions.

"This way," he said as he motioned to the funeral home employees that they needed to go upstairs. The two employees, clean-shaven and dressed in dark gray suits, walked up the stairs in front of him. They hesitated at the top of the stairs until Alston pointed toward the room where Eliza lay in bed. "She almost looks like she's just sleeping," Alston whispered.

Eliza lay peacefully on the bed before them. Her head tilted toward the window as if she was daydreaming. Alston walked around the men to stand by his sister's side. He brushed back the hair that had fallen across her eyes and then placed his hand on her face. Tears rolled down his cheeks as he prepared to say goodbye to Eliza.

"Please, take good care of her. She's my little sister."

"Mr. Alston, you might want to step out while we get her ready to go," the younger man said.

Alston nodded and walked to his bedroom. As he closed the door, he heard the sound of the gurney wheels as they brought it up the stairs. Falling to his knees, Alston lowered his head into his hands and sobbed.

***

"This is just heartbreaking," Lizzie whispered, careful not to disturb the other researchers. "Have you been able to find anything in the newspaper yet or should I keep going?"

"I did locate a small obituary. It's not written like those you read today. When you are looking through the obits, don't set your expectations too high. Sometimes they contain a lot of detail about the person, but most times the obituaries for the average person in our county were no more than a line or two." Gertrude waved Lizzie over to her machine. "This is Eliza's." She pointed to the bottom of a column in the newspaper to a short column simple titled, *Death Announcements.*

Eliza James, daughter of Frank and Amelia James, died at the home of her brother, Alston, last week. Services were held at the First Baptist Church. Rev. Thomas Ray officiated.

"Is there any way to find out what happened to her?" Lizzie kept reading the words over and over. "I'm just shocked that they summed up her life in a few little sentences."

"I asked my father what happened to his sister just once. He always believed that she died of a broken heart," said Gertrude. "That's all he would say."

"What do you think she died of that day?" Lizzie asked while writing on her notepad.

"I think he was right. There is a real syndrome nicknamed the 'broken heart syndrome'. It's a type of cardiomyopathy caused by deep emotional stress. Think of it as a form of a heart attack but lighter. I think it's fitting. Daddy didn't realize that decades later they would determine that a broken heart is a real medical condition."

"That's so sad, Gran. Poor Eliza."

Lizzie's heart grieved for the aunt that she would never know. "Out of curiosity, do you know what happened to Eldridge's body? Did they bury him in the town cemetery?"

"During that time, the cemetery was segregated by race. Eldridge was buried on the other side of the fence from our family plot in what was designated as the 'colored cemetery'." Gertrude squeezed her lips together in a frown and shook her head slowly. "Different times, indeed."

The other gals had already left, their research completed. Only Lizzie and Gertrude remained in the dark, cool room. Lizzie bent down and placed her arm around her grandmother's shoulders. "Would you take me to visit her grave tomorrow? I'd like to pay my respects."

"I think that would be a wonderful idea." Gertrude smiled. "You'll find this interesting. Eliza's headstone faces a different direction compared to those around her. Wouldn't it be something if Daddy did it so that she could face Eldridge? I can't imagine the attention that would have caused. He also put an angel on her headstone. I had no idea why until I read the he found her beneath the weeping angel that night."

"I want to look through a few more newspapers first, though. Are you sure that there aren't any other mentions of the lynching?" Lizzie asked.

"What you found is most likely all you will find, but we can keep looking if you'd like. It's always best to exhaust all your resources."

The two women looked through several issues of the town newspaper without result before Gertrude suggested that they try the archives of the larger paper one town north of Everett Springs.

"Gran! This article lists information about a gathering for the KKK in the area the night after the Eldridge was murdered. Do you think those men could have been involved in what happened to the two of them?"

"Like I mentioned before, my father was worried about the KKK, though we will have no way of knowing if it was them. According to the diary, Eliza was never able to give him too many details about the men that were there that night. She did seem to refer to her main attacker as the man in white, so I would assume they could have been involved." Gertrude removed her reading glasses and rubbed her straining eyes. "I don't know what you'll be able to find out. Their ranks are extremely secretive. They kept their faces hidden for a reason."

"Because they were cowards," Lizzie said under her breath.

"Lizzie, darling, are you sure you want to dig into this hornet's nest? You might not like where it leads."

"If I had a chance to expose those responsible and to shine a light on their evil, I would do it in a heartbeat. I'm a big girl. I think I'll take my chances."

As Lizzie gathered her things, she thought about the ages of those involved. She knew that most of the people involved wouldn't be alive, but she hoped she'd have the chance to confront them if they were.

***

Leaving Gertrude to finish her other research, Lizzie headed home. As she walked across the grassy yard in front of the library, Avery Abernathy walked out of the local diner.

"Hey, Avery!" Lizzie called as she jogged to meet him on the sidewalk. "Imagine running into you in the same parking lot twice in the same day. How's your day with your grandfather going?"

"We're having a good time catching up. Actually, I wanted to talk to you. My grandfather said that you were looking into a family diary of yours. Finding anything good?"

"I am indeed. It was my grandmother's little trick to get me involved in her family history research. Unfortunately for me, it worked." Lizzie said with a giggle. "The diary tells a tragic story in my family's past, so it's been an emotional week."

"I'm sorry to hear that. I hope it wasn't something crazy like a crime." Avery hoped to lead her into a conversation about the details. Any information she shared would give him insight into her intentions. Avery shifted his weight and leaned against the newspaper box next to him. He crossed his arms loosely over his chest and tilted his head to the side. He wanted to appear relaxed and hide the nerves that he felt.

"Actually, there was. My aunt and her companion were murdered. I'm determined to find out as much information about what happened as I can."

"You're making it sound like you're the modern day Nancy Drew," he teased.

"She was a white girl dating a black boy in the south during the 1930s. It didn't go over well as you can imagine. He was lynched, and I think she was raped. I can't prove a lot, but the timing and notes make me believe the local KKK had a hand in it." Lizzie fiddled with her keys. "I can't prove anything yet, but I feel like I need to bring justice to my aunt's name if I can. It's hard to think we had such darkness and horror in our little slice of Georgia heaven, but we did. Those people were just evil. I need to know who was involved."

"Do you think they would still be alive? What's the chance in that?"

"I'm sure you're right. I'd just like to find an answer for once. Tragedy seems to be a theme in my family tree. It just doesn't end." Lizzie dropped her head to avoid making eye contact with Avery, but he could still see the tears starting to well up in her eyes.

He wasn't sure how to react. He couldn't breathe easy until he knew that his grandfather's good name was protected. Avery shifted his weight from one side to the other and looked at Lizzie's eyes before speaking. "Sometimes we just want closure. That's what I hear you say. Right? Maybe there are other ways you can get it that might be more realistic than to track down the people involved." Avery said a silent prayer as he waited for her answer.

"I suppose that's true. I know that it sounds crazy to chase something like this after all these years. I should be going. Besides, if I keep you too long your grandfather will kill me!"

Avery cringed at her choice of words. *"If you only knew what you just said..."*

***

After a long day of researching, Lizzie was thankful to see Jack busy at the kitchen when she walked in.

"I thought it would be a great night for comfort food," said Jack. Still holding the cast iron pan handle in one hand and his spatula in the other, he leaned over and kissed his wife hello. "Now don't distract me while I'm creating perfection." He turned his attention back to his task creating of his specialty. Lizzie loved his grilled cheese sandwich with bacon, mayonnaise, and a little Dijon mustard.

Lizzie's mouth watered. "Don't let me take your attention, sir. Food is love, and I could use a dose of it tonight." She set her things down on the kitchen table and folded into the barstool behind the kitchen island. "It was a crazy day today. I never realized that researching could take it out of you, but it does."

"Oh, yeah? Do tell. What exciting adventure did you take while I was hard at work today?"

"I learned to use a microfilm reader. Jealous?" teased Lizzie.

"Boring…" Jack yawned and patted his mouth with the kitchen mitt.

"Ok, try this one. I met Thomas Abernathy's grandson."

"Now, that's interesting. What's his story?"

"He's down visiting from Atlanta. He wanted to check out Everett Springs. His mom and dad moved out of town after he was born, and he's thinking about moving back. He seems nice. He's our age. You should meet him."

"Why don't you invite him over for dinner while he's here?"

"That's a great idea. We could fire up the barbecue."

Jack flipped another sandwich onto a plate and slid it in front of Lizzie before reaching into the oven for a pan of spicy sweet potato fries. "Did you find out anything about Eliza and Eldridge?"

Lizzie started twirling a chunk of hair around the index finger of her right hand. "Do you know what bothers me most about this story? It could be anyone. This is only a few generations from me, so the people who did this to Eldridge and Eliza could have descendants in town right alongside me." Lizzie paused. "What if I know the people involved? Do you think that's possible?" She ripped a corner off of the sandwich and took a bite loaded with cheese and bacon.

"Anything's possible. Would it make a difference to you?" Jack kept tending to his grilled cheese. The sound of the spatula scraping on the cast iron skillet creaked in the background.

"I don't know how it wouldn't. It just seems so hard to reconcile that it was happening here of all places. It was in our hometown, Jack. It's just so cruel." Lizzie swiped a handful of sweet potato fries through the ketchup that Jack had squirted onto her plate. "If I did know them, I don't know if I could forgive them for something like this."

"Your Gran reminded you that it was a different time. Don't forget that it isn't your burden to bear either. You didn't know these two. I know that sounds harsh, but it's the reality. Forgiveness comes in all forms, especially if you aren't the one involved. You wouldn't have anything to forgive, would you?"

"Jack, I can't believe it's that simple for you. When you are the cause of someone's death, you don't deserve forgiveness. Every person involved in lynching was responsible for the deaths of two people. If it hadn't been for their actions that night Eliza and Eldridge would have been alive. Two families were ruined that night." Lizzie stood up from the table and picked up her glass of sweet tea. "I've got to get some air."

"Lizzie, come on now...."

Lizzie didn't hear him. She let the screen door slam against the frame as she walked onto the back porch. The idea of giving forgiveness to anyone in her own life who was capable of a crime like this felt so foreign. Like a wind coming from the middle of a tornado, her breath was taken away as she began to understand the reality of what she said. What if it was someone in her life today?

The concept of forgiveness was such a hard one to Lizzie. She carried a heavy resentment against herself for her part in the death of her parents. If she hadn't begged to be at the church that night they wouldn't have had a reason to be in the car. Instead, they were driving in the storm that destroyed her family. She couldn't forgive herself.

Lizzie looked up at the night sky and started thinking about the lives that were destroyed that night in the cemetery. Tears began to well up inside of her. There are some things in this world that are just unforgivable, she thought. "I'll never forgive them."

After Lizzie composed herself, she returned to the kitchen.

Jack walked over to his wife and wrapped his arms around her. "You know I love you, right?"

Lizzie just sighed. This was Jack's way of telling her that she was in need of a change in her attitude.

"You really need to think about forgiving yourself for something you couldn't control. It wasn't your fault, you know. You're letting it get in the way of your other relationships and the way you think of people. You've got such a negative opinion and you need to remember that people are capable of change and redemption. I promise."

"That's what you keep saying." Lizzie pulled away from her husband's embrace and returned to her seat.

"Then it must be true," he said as he pulled both plates out of the oven where they had been kept warm. "Now eat."

Without another word, the two ate in peace as Lizzie thought about what her husband said. She still didn't think that she needed forgiveness, but she would consider offering it up to others.

CHAPTER SEVENTEEN

After returning home from the diner, Thomas needed to lie down. Avery wanted to keep the house quiet, so he chose to sit in the backyard while his grandfather slept. He needed to decide what to do about the situation that threatened his family. His grandfather was one of the most peace-loving individuals that he knew. The people in town and of the church knew him as a loving person who was there to help and give. Avery had to make sure that his memory was kept intact. Thomas Abernathy was getting older. He couldn't let his legacy be one of violence. His name had to be kept away from the events that took the lives of Eldridge and Eliza.

As he sat in the old, wooden deck chair, he looked across the back fence taking in the surroundings. The Abernathy farm had been in his grandfather's family for the last two hundred years. As the sun set, Avery looked over the crops growing high in the fields. As a child, he would run through those fields, ducking between rows of corn or jumping over melons on the vine. Memories of childhood began fading to the nightmares of the past and of Greer Abernathy. The secrets held in that dirt went back generations and had to be kept quiet. He didn't want them unearthed.

His mind wandered to his great-grandfather. Greer was a mystery to him. Avery couldn't remember a single story or memory shared by his family that included his great-grandfather. There were no childhood tales passed down from his mother about time spent with her grandfather. Greer was a person who lived as he wanted. Tall and thick in build, he didn't allow others to speak against him or his ideas. He was rough and loud with everyone that he encountered, especially his children and wife.

Avery's grandfather took the opposite approach with his small family. Quiet and caring, Thomas tried to support and love his children and grandchildren. He made it a point to avoid confrontation. He married and lived a quiet life rooted in the church and the community that he loved. As the youngest in the family, he never expected to inherit his father's farm until his older brother was killed. A soldier in the fields of Europe during World War II, his brother never made it home. Reluctantly, his great-grandfather changed his will to leave the land to young Thomas. Over the years, Thomas grew apart from his remaining family until none remained. Avery assumed the space in his family was from a difference of opinions or beliefs. He never would have guessed that the root was in the guilt that his grandfather revealed.

He spent the next hour pulling back the curtain on memories hoping to find a clue to explain how his parents could hide this horror from him. "So that's why we moved," he thought. The weight of his new reality sat on Avery's chest. His family had been responsible for the lynching of a young African American man and the rape and death of a local girl. If they didn't live in the area it made it that much harder for Avery to learn the truth.

Avery reached into his pocket for his cell phone. He glanced at his watch to check the time. "Still early." He could reach his mother before she settled in for the evening. Dialing the number, he realized that he had to let her know what was going on.

"Hello, dear," his mother answered. "How's the vacation with Granddaddy? Are you figuring out if you'd like to stay in Everett Springs or not?"

"It's been interesting, that's for sure. I haven't decided yet about moving. There are some things that I have to sort out first." He stopped to choose the right words.

"Avery, are you all right?" his mother asked.

"I've been wrestling with something today that I think we might need to discuss. Granddaddy told me about the incident with Greer and the young boy Eldridge. Mama, he told me about his involvement. What's worse is that I've met a descendant of Eliza's, and she's asking questions."

His mother went quiet on the other end of the phone. "Oh, son. This isn't how I wanted you to learn about this. I didn't want you to know. Whatever you do, remember that it is in the past and it needs to stay there. That's not Granddaddy's life now. It's not who he is."

"I know, Mama. I'm not upset with him. Honest. I'm just worried is all. I'm worried about Lizzie. That's her name - Lizzie."

"The Clydell girl? I don't understand. What's she doing asking about this? Does she know about it? Oh Avery, that will kill your grandfather. He adores her so."

"The girl from that night was Lizzie's great-aunt. She's digging to find out who was involved. I have to figure out how I'm going to keep it from coming out. It seems like the story is rearing its ugly head once again, and I need to stay here until it's stopped."

Avery walked over to the bright red metal gate that divided the front pasture from the back. Leaning over it, he rested his arms and head on the top rung. "I just don't know how to make that happen."

"You can't run from the truth, Avery. I've tried. It may have taken a few decades, but you still found out."

"The truth is what scares me, Mama."

"Reach out to her for forgiveness. That's all you can do."

"What if that isn't enough, Mama?" he asked. "What then?"

***

Following Thomas' nap, the two men enjoyed the type of country meal that Avery remembered from his childhood. They stuffed themselves with fried chicken, mashed potatoes and gravy, and enough biscuits to last them until spring. After they finished, Avery cleared the dinner plates and silverware from the table. Thomas stretched and shuffled into the other room. Still drained after their earlier conversation at the diner, his movements were heavy and slow. Pouring his heart and sadness into his grandson had been a harder experience than he had expected. It had been years since he dragged up the details of that day. Hearing himself say the words caused him to relive the events. Thomas saw the pain in Eliza's face as the men violated her. He heard the screams of Eldridge as he watched his love get beaten and broken. The demons awoke, and they weren't letting the old man walk away without damage. His rest didn't provide the respite that they had hoped it would.

Standing at the kitchen sink rinsing dishes, Avery thought about his next move. He wasn't used to thinking about people as threats, but that's what Lizzie felt like. A panic welled up inside him and took over his body raising his blood pressure and heightening his anxiety. He couldn't stop thinking of Lizzie Clydell and the pain that flashed in her eyes as she told him the story of her great aunt. She seemed so determined to locate the truth. As he thought of Lizzie's words, his blood began to boil. The muscles in his neck and jaw tensed as he thought of the young woman who held his grandfather's fate in her hands. He wasn't sure if his anger would continue, and perhaps he didn't care. His hands shook and caused the soapy china dish he held crashed to the ground.

"Avery? You okay, son?" asked Thomas from the great room.

"Sorry about the plate. I was just thinking, Gramps. I'll clean it up."

The phone rang, breaking the heavy silence. Before Avery could pick up the heavy black receiver from its wall mount he heard his grandfather answer from the extension.

"Well, hello there my dear. How are you this evening?" Thomas paused as the other unidentified party continued. "Aren't you the sweetest? We'd be glad to come for dinner tomorrow. Avery will still be here. Can we bring anything? I can make some biscuits if you'd like."

Avery crept around the corner for a closer listen. He could hear the tone in his grandfather's voice change, reflecting a little nervousness. Just as curiosity got hold of him, he heard his grandfather disconnect the call with a pleasantry.

"So, which girlfriend invited you over?" Avery teased, hoping to lighten the mood.

"That was Lizzie Clydell inviting us over for dinner tomorrow night. Avery, what will I do if she's found out?" Thomas lowered his head into his hand and began to weep. "She's so precious to me. Her grandmother is like family, and that little girl has filled a place in my heart that became so empty when your mama left town. What will I do if I lose her after she knows the truth? Your mama couldn't face me when she found out about what my father did. What if it's the same with Lizzie? What do I do now?"

Avery walked over to his grandfather and joined him on the vintage settee. The old piece of furniture creaked as the two men sat side by side. Avery realized that after today their roles had become reversed. No longer was his grandfather patting the back of a scared boy assuring him that everything would be fine. It was Avery's turn to give his grandfather words of comfort.

"I'll make sure it's okay, Gramps. Just trust me. I won't let anything happen." Avery hoped that he wasn't lying. "I'm sure she doesn't know or she wouldn't invite us. It will be fine. I promise."

As he walked into the kitchen to finish the after dinner chores, he noticed a photo on the wall. It was a wedding photo of new love. A young groom stood tall and thin in his best clothes wearing a look of accomplishment on his face. He was smiling, proud to be a new husband. His wife, delicate and small, stood next to him, her head barely reaching his shoulder. Her lips curled up toward her bright, wide eyes she held fixed on her husband. Her bridal headdress was made from a simple lace that was pinned in her hair and draped just behind her. Her hands lifted to her chest in order to hold her wedding flowers so the camera could capture the beautiful blooms. The groom gently held one of her hands to help support the weight of the bouquet while his other arm wrapped around her back. Their young faces seemed so full of hope and innocence.

"Gramps, who's this?" Avery was drawn into the image. He assumed it was his grandfather and grandmother as it took a position of prominence in the room. He was surprised that he had never noticed the heavy wooden frame with the thick beveled glass before. "Is this you and Granny?"

"Believe it or not, that's my father and mother on their wedding day." Thomas looked up at his parents not with the face of an old man but the eyes of a child. "My father was innocent once. I'm not sure what happened to turn him into the monster that he would become later on. I love this photo because it makes me think that life could have been different if only he had kept that innocence. He had a heart that could love once. If only he had found the ability to give grace to others instead of sorrow." His weak voice trailed off. "Don't hate me, Avery. Don't hate me for what my father did."

Avery stood with his grandfather and stared at the photo. He couldn't believe that the face before him was that of Greer Abernathy, KKK member and the man that would ruin the lives of so many. "Lord be with me so I don't become him," he thought. From that moment on, Avery decided that appealing to Lizzie's heart of forgiveness would be the only way to approach the situation.

"We need to ask for grace, Gramps. That's all we can do."

Avery knew then what he had to do. He needed to reach out to Lizzie and try to bring peace between their families before pain grew into hatred like it had all those generations before. He had to do it for himself as much as he did for Lizzie. Avery couldn't allow the evil that lived in Greer to live in him, and grace was the only way to stop it.

CHAPTER EIGHTEEN

The sun glared into Lizzie's eyes as she parked the truck in the gravel lot next to the cemetery. "I hope this isn't too steep for you to get out, Gran," she said fought against gravity to push the heavy metal door open.

"You worry too much. I'm old but I'm not weak," said Gertrude.

Lizzie laughed as she stretched her back with her hands rested on her hips. She had been hesitant when her grandmother suggested they make a run to the cemetery before the barbecue, but the timing was perfect.

"I guess if you have to spend a morning in the cemetery, it's best to do it on a sunny one," said Lizzie.

"That's how I know you haven't been bitten by the bug yet."

"What do you mean?" Lizzie shaded her eyes with her hands as she looked toward her grandmother.

"Once you're hooked, it doesn't matter if it's sunny. You'll hunt for your dead in a thunderstorm if you have to just to get the facts off the headstone."

The two women started walking up the path toward the cemetery. Lizzie offered her elbow as support but Gertrude refused. Bright sun showed through gaps in the trees where leaves were starting to fall. The fall was always her favorite time of year. This season had been particularly dry, so the leaves that dropped crunched under her feet. Bright golds, oranges, and reds mixed on the ground into a pile so colorful that it caught her attention.

Lizzie found herself day dreaming about the many falls spent playing in the leaves with her father. He would rake the leaves just so he could watch his daughter jump into pile after pile as she laughed. She could still see her mother's smiling face looking through the window from behind the curtains. Grace Hines thought she was catching a private moment between them, but both Elton and Lizzie knew she was watching. They let her have her secret, and they kept theirs.

Snapping herself out of the past, Lizzie looked forward toward the hillside where the town's dead had been laid to rest. As a general rule, she tried to avoid this place. It reminded her of the life she had lost and put her into a bad mindset. The sadness started to creep into Lizzie's chest. "Stay focused." There was a time to mourn for her parents, and today wasn't it.

"Where are we headed, Gran?" she asked.

"We need to go over there. That was the section he'd be in, not here with our kin." Gertrude pointed a finger beyond the fence. Gertrude pulled out her map where she had marked a few potential locations for Eldridge's grave and began walking toward the second section of burial plots.

As they made their way through the larger section of the cemetery to the second gate, they wandered through row after row of headstones. The plots belonging to families with wealth were embellished with stones heavy in beautiful detail. Lizzie saw scrolls, crosses, and even unique stones carved to look like log stumps. Large spires and obelisks stood tall among smaller, more delicate slabs of stone. These contrasted with the stones of the older inhabitants which tilted and leaned as the ground around them settled. Despite their differences, each marker still bore witness to the life they represented.

Lizzie and Gertrude crossed through the rickety gate that separated the old African American section from the original cemetery. The walking path wasn't cleared of heavy rocks and vines as they had been from the ground in other sections of the cemetery.

"The headstones look so different here," said Lizzie. She noticed that the stones were rougher in design. Many included only initials and dates that looked as if someone chiseled them with common tools. Some were simply blank with no name to represent the life that was lost. They were a stark contrast to the others made by tradesmen who considered this type of work art. Row after row of headstones looked the same. Broken. Rough. Worn. The difference between the two sides of the fence was heartbreaking.

"I just didn't imagine it would look different," said Lizzie. Like many of her generation, the idea that society separated and labeled individuals as better or less was foreign to her. The concept was one in her history book. It wasn't supposed to be so accessible in her own town.

"A lot of things were different. It just doesn't seem real until you see it for yourself. Imagine being a grieving family and knowing that you had to be buried on this side of the fence just because of your skin color." Gertrude stood looking across the cemetery. "This is why I need people to work with me on this cemetery, dear. They were treated so poorly in life. We have to protect them in death. If this cemetery is destroyed who will remember them?"

Lizzie wound through the haphazard rows of graves with her grandmother. Finally, they found what they had come for: the headstone of Eldridge Reeves. It was a simple stone decorated with only a roughly carved cross followed by his name and date of death underneath. His grave sat between the graves of other families with no other Reeves names appearing near.

"There's no family near him." Lizzie's heart sank. "Why is he buried all alone?"

"It could be that there weren't any plots near his ancestors or perhaps this is where they had room at the time. He was likely the first to die in his family. His parents would most likely have been living. He was quite young, remember?" The headstone was overgrown from lack of care. Gertrude knelt down to clear the leaves and weeds from around the headstone. Lizzie bent to help her grandmother.

"Did you ever find out what happened to his parents?" asked Lizzie.

"His family left the county after his death. I can't blame them. It wasn't safe for them to stay. The memory had to be painful." Gertrude wiped the dirt from her hands on a handkerchief that she had pulled from her back pocket. "I couldn't begin to imagine the fear that they held, or the anger when they would walk through town not knowing. They would never know if they were coming face to face with his murderers on any given day. It was hard on my parents every day. It had to be the same for his family, only they had added danger. They couldn't say anything or they could have been next. It was a dark time, Lizzie. A dark time indeed."

Lizzie wondered if they wrestled with looks of pity from their community as she did after her parents' death. Now that it had been two decades, people had stopped identifying her as the child whose parents had died. How long would the town have identified them as the parents of a murdered son? It couldn't have been easy to live in that shadow of cruelty, scandal, and loss.

"I'll take care of your grave, Eldridge. I'll be your family now." Lizzie knelt by the stone and said a prayer, determined to promise God that she would not let him be forgotten. "Don't worry. I'll always remember, as will my children after me."

Gertrude leaned near and rested her head on Lizzie's shoulder. "That's my girl."

The two walked through the cemetery gate and moved back into the section of the cemetery that held their ancestors. They crossed through the section that held the town's founders and into the section that held the graves of Gertrude's parents. They stopped in front of the joint headstone for Alston and Anne James. The wide marker spanned both graves and held their birth, marriage, and death dates.

Gertrude walked up to the stone and placed her hand along the top edge. "If my daddy could only see us now," she said, lifting her eyes to the heavens as her voice trailed off.

To the left of Alston's final resting place was the headstone of the young Eliza James. Several small statues of angels surrounded the base of the headstone, each with their head bent as if in mourning. Lizzie noticed the intricate design that adorned the corners of the stone. In the center was her inscription:

Eliza Gertrude James
1919-1934
Daughter, Sister, Friend
"Taken from us too soon"

Lizzie stood still, looking at the headstone of her great-aunt, the mysterious Eliza. "I am so sorry this happened to you," Lizzie whispered.

"I think we would have liked her," said Gertrude.

Lizzie lifted her eyes to reply to her grandmother. Instead, she caught sight of the twisted and bare branches of a tree near the bank of the creek just beyond the final rows of headstones.

"Unbelievable. Gran, look. That has to be it."

Lizzie ran over to the tree, jumping around rows of graves, and placed her hand on its trunk. She could almost feel the hatred that had burned scars into the bark. Titling her head toward the sky, she could see damage to the tree limbs, the gashes ripped out of the wood as if they were bleeding wounds from inside the tree itself. She was certain that a place couldn't hold onto emotion, but this place seemed to exude it.

"Why would they leave it standing?" she asked her grandmother, not expecting an answer.

Lizzie started reliving the details she had read in Alston's diary. Images flashed in her mind. She saw the creek bank where Eliza had been so roughly shoved into the water and the branch where Eldridge had finally lost his life. She turned toward her grandmother, her eyes begging for Gertrude to help her make sense of what she saw. Then she saw it. Just a few rows in front of them sat a weeping angel. Lizzie knew that there stood the place where her great-aunt's heart broke. It was the angel that Alston had written about that night.

Lizzie couldn't focus. Her eyes became hazy and her ears grew quiet as the horrors of the location screamed out tears for Eliza. Her legs became weak as she struggled to process the events that took place where she stood almost a century before. Lizzie cried like the weeping angel who lay with her arms and head across the headstone where Alston found his sister. Within seconds, she was on her hands and knees begging God for understanding as Gertrude clutched her by the shoulders.

She could hear Gertrude whispering in her ear. "Breathe, child. You've got to breathe."

Lizzie clung to the grass and earth looking for a place to release her anger. She needed a place to scream and something to rage against. Lizzie's cries became louder turning into screams as they released into the air around her. She wept for innocence. She wept for the loss of life and love. Lizzie could no longer hold in the emotions that bubbled up through the pages of the diary. She screamed for the anger and fear that entered her great-grandfather's life that day. As the emotions took over, she realized she cried for something else. Lizzie also wept for her own loss.

"Gran! I'm so sorry. I don't know what came over me." Ashamed, Lizzie dropped her eyes and whispered an apology.

"Don't think anything about it. You need to let it out. That's what we were hoping for. You've got to finally let it all out." Gertrude hugged her granddaughter close.

Lizzie began to compose herself enough to stand. It wasn't until she brushed the dry grass and crushed leaves from her clothing did she realize that she had collapsed onto the ground. Looking towards the sunset, she realized it was time to go home to Jack.

"Look at the time. Mr. Thomas and Avery will be over to the house soon. I guess we better head back. I just want to make one more stop before we go."

The two walked hand in hand past the graves of Eliza, Alston, and Anne until they came to the graves of her parents, Elton and Grace Hines. Looking at the shared date of death, Lizzie began to cry soft tears despite the emotional exhaustion that she felt. Gertrude began cleaning the weeds and grass from around the base of the headstone as she had done with each stone they visited that day.

"Your father never did like to keep his room tidy," Gertrude whispered with a little giggle. She looked up at her granddaughter standing beside her and smiled. "They loved you dearly."

Lizzie smiled and knew that her grandmother was telling her the truth. She kissed her hand lightly and placed it on top of her mother's name that was engraved into the marble headstone.

"I'll visit again soon. I just can't stay today," Lizzie whispered. "You may have been taken from me, but at least you weren't taken from each other."

The two women walked in silence toward the parking lot while each wiped the tears from her eyes. When they reached the bottom of the hill, Lizzie turned toward the cemetery one last time. She stood in silent remembrance for a moment before opening the car door for her grandmother. They settled in for the short drive home, neither saying a word until they reached their destination.

CHAPTER NINETEEN

Lizzie hurried around the kitchen preparing for the arrival of their dinner guests. The warm evening was perfect for grilling out, yet still cool enough to warrant lighting the fire pit for ambiance. Lizzie added candles and candy dishes throughout the outdoor seating area as Jack prepared his steak and chicken for cooking. The two hurried to finish last minute preparations before their guests arrived. Wanting to introduce Avery to the group, Lizzie had invited her grandmother and the gals.

"It looks great, babe. They'll love it," she said as she walked by Jack's counter of meat and sauce.

Just then, Gertrude and her friends arrived. After a bevy of hugs and kisses, the ladies joined Lizzie inside to gather drinks before the Abernathy men arrived.

"Remember, dear, there's no talk about the diary tonight. We agreed." Gertrude wanted a light-hearted evening filled with laughter not sorrow. "I know you're focused on it right now, but it can't control every aspect of conversation. Have you decided to go back to the Center next week?"

"You make it sound like I've become obsessed." Lizzie laughed. "Isn't this what you wanted when you dragged me to your meeting?"

"Well, friend, it isn't that we don't care. It's just that we're bored," Blue said with a wink as she carried a tray of serving plates out to Jack at the grill.

Everyone laughed but Claud, who rolled her eyes.

"What she means is that there are many things to discuss," said Abi, softening the words of her friend. "Perhaps pulling up an event like this of the past isn't the best dinner conversation. That's all, Lizzie. We've got a new guest who may like to talk about something else."

"A new guest who wants to talk about what?" Avery Abernathy asked as he walked into the kitchen.

"Avery! Good, you made it. Have you met everyone?" Lizzie introduced their guest to the group. Each woman gave him a hug in true family fashion just as Thomas walked in carrying a plate of his famous biscuits.

"I'm not interrupting some juicy gossip meant only for the ladies, am I?" said Avery.

"My grandmother's cronies are trying to convince me that you won't want to hear the legends and lore of our family's past. I think it might make for interesting conversation. It's filled with sadness and history. Things we all can relate to, don't you think?"

Lizzie walked over to the refrigerator for drinks. "Who's having lemonade and who's having tea?" She opened the door and peeked inside, trying to locate the fresh drinks that she made. "Jack has the grill so I get the easy stuff like drinks and sides. I got the better end of the deal."

After gathering the drinks and sides, the group made their way to the back patio to visit. Questions about Avery and his family led the discussion. He told of his job and his home, but also how he wanted to be closer to his grandfather. Living out of town was harder, he said, now that Thomas was aging.

"I'm not so old that I can't hear you over there, boy," Thomas teased. "He thinks I'm unable to care for myself. Next thing you know I'll have him living with me as a babysitter."

"I think you'd enjoy it, wouldn't you Mr. Thomas? You must like the idea of Avery moving closer." Lizzie passed a tray of appetizers around for the group to enjoy. "You don't have much family here anymore, do you?"

"No, I don't unfortunately. My brother was killed in the service, and my only child is Avery's mama. I tease him but it would be nice to have family nearby. That's all that is important." Thomas leaned forward and patted Avery's knee.

Without warning, Lizzie felt a melancholy that fall over her.

"Are you all right, Lizzie girl?" Thomas asked?

"I'm just thinking about what you said. My family is so important to me. Unfortunately, we're a small lot, too. It's just me, Jack, and Gran now." She looked over at her grandmother and gave her a sheepish smile. Jack planted a kiss on the top of her head then walked into the house for more grilling supplies before finishing the task at hand.

"I'm sorry, I didn't even think about that my dear," Thomas replied.

Lizzie saw the confused look on Avery's face. "A car accident killed my parents when I was a child. It was my fault," she said as she fought back the tears.

"No, it wasn't, and you need to stop blaming yourself. You were just a child," Gertrude said. "Thomas, tell her. Children aren't responsible for things like that. Accidents just happen."

The color drained from Thomas' face. Tears welled up in his eyes. "No," he said as he wiped his eyes. "I can't do that, Gertrude."

Lizzie had never heard her friend speak as harshly to her grandmother as he just did. His voice cracked with a combination of sorrow and anger. It was a feeling that Lizzie understood well. She knew that there was something else under the surface that was bothering him. She was just unable to tell what it was.

"Are you okay, Mr. Thomas?" Lizzie perched on the edge of her chair unsure of what she should do next. She looked at Avery who shared the same terrified expression. "I feel like I'm missing something."

"Lizzie," Thomas started, "sometimes children do cause problems that they don't realize. They don't always have control over the events around them, just as your grandmother said. The guilt can still follow them around for decades. I just don't know how else to say it. I have that same guilt. I'm guilty." Thomas collapsed his head into his hands and sobbed. All eyes sat on him, and no one knew quite what to do.

"Well, isn't this a quick twist in the evening's story line," Blue whispered to Abi who shushed her old friend. "What? It's true, isn't it?"

"It's my fault, Gertrude. It's all my fault. Please forgive me," Thomas cried as he walked to his old friend, begging for forgiveness. He picked up her hands into his and continued to cry.

"What's your fault, Thomas?" Gertrude said hesitantly as she looked at the group. "We've been friends a long time, and you've never done anything against me. You're talking foolishness. Everything is fine."

"No, it's not. I did it. I killed Eldridge and Eliza."

Lizzie gasped and dropped the glass of lemonade in her hand sending shards of glass everywhere. The group started talking at once. Gertrude pulled her hand away and whispered something under her breath that Lizzie couldn't quite hear. Jack came running over with a broom and dust pan. By his expression Lizzie knew that he hadn't been privy to any of the conversation. His wide eyes searched her face for signs of her emotions. Lizzie sat in shock as she listened to the noise around her. Thomas, a man that she loved and respected from the time she was a little girl, had admitted to having a part in the murder of two teenagers. All at once she felt pain, sadness, and anger.

Avery stood in the center of the group and raised his hands as if to protect his grandfather. "I think this conversation is a little misunderstanding. That's not what my grandfather meant. I think that we might need to back up a little bit."

"Let's just calm down for a moment," Claud said. "Blue, honey, do something," she whispered to her friend sitting next to her.

Blue shifted in her seat as she attempted to stand. "You didn't want me to talk, remember?" Claud's jaw dropped. "Well, make up your mind."

The room sat in silence. Lizzie looked at Thomas, tears welling up in her eyes. "You mean you were there? You were with them that night?" She paused for a moment, taking in the full weight of his statement. "It can't be you. If it was you, then that means you're the one that I've been searching for. That means you're the one that I've had nightmares about. You're the murderer."

Before she realized what she was doing, Lizzie was standing in front of the fire pit looking into the eyes of the elderly man. On instinct, Avery stood to match her movement. He moved closer to Lizzie, touching her lightly on the arm in an attempt to move her away from his grandfather. Without a sound, Jack stood to face Avery, ready to make a move should the young man get too rough with his wife. Blue walked to Lizzie's side. Patting her back, she guided Lizzie to her chair without a sound.

"It's all my fault," Thomas said as he wept into his weathered hands. "I heard Mr. Alston praying in the church. I asked my father what it meant to have hidden secrets. He made me tell him the entire story, which I did. I was a child and did what I was told. If I didn't, my daddy would have beaten me. I was afraid. I had no idea that he was going to do what he did."

Avery pulled a chair next to his grandfather and took a seat. "Just listen to him, please," he begged Lizzie. His eyes softened as he placed a hand on his grandfather's back. "Just tell them what happened, Gramps."

Thomas took a deep breath and began again. "After my father learned what I knew, he went to find Eldridge. I didn't realize he was hunting for them until we were in the truck driving around town. My father made me sit in the middle of the seat between him and my older brother."

"The one who passed in the War?" Claud whispered to Blue who sat next to her again.

"It turned out to be his initiation into the Klan. I was still young, so I was only made to watch. I remember my mother screaming not to take us. She was clawing at my daddy as he piled me into the car. I saw him back-hand her across the face, and she fell into the dirt. She kept screaming for him to stop. I can still hear her voice trail off as we drove down the road. I heard her calling on the name of God, begging for Him to bring her baby back."

Just then, Jack walked out of the house with a box of tissues for the ladies and a clean handkerchief for Thomas. Lizzie thanked him and realized that she hadn't even noticed him leaving. She stared into the fire as it danced, leaving trails of light flashes in her eyes. She heard the group asking Thomas questions, but none of the words made sense.

"I can't believe it was you. I worried that I'd know a murderer, but I never thought it would be you." Lizzie turned to look at him. "You've preached love and Lord to me all my life, but you killed two innocent teenagers. How could you take someone's life and then still be close to our family?" Tears streamed down Lizzie's face, catching her hair in sticky tangles around her cheeks. "You betrayed me, yet you come to my house year after year, and you see me Sunday after Sunday. You look me in the eyes at church and tell me that you love me. How could you after what you've done?"

"Gramps, I think that's enough," said Avery as he scrambled to his feet. "We have to go. Say goodnight. We've got to get out of here." Avery tried to rush his grandfather onto his feet as panic flooded his chest. A fight or flight response was kicking in, and he had to leave fast. He looked around the seating area into the faces of women he barely knew and wondered what was going to be next.

Abi sat next to Gertrude who remained silent. She patted her friend's hand and glanced at Claud who was again whispering a prayer. Even Blue sat speechless at the new revelation. Avery thanked Jack and gathered his grandfather's jacket.

As they were walking toward the side porch, Thomas Abernathy grabbed his chest in pain. His face tensed as panic washed across his eyes.

"Gramps, what's wrong?" screamed Avery.

Within seconds it became clear to those in the yard what was happening. Thomas Abernathy was having a heart attack.

"Jack, call 911!" Lizzie screamed. She was immediately faced with a choice. Did she hate the man who destroyed her family or did she pray for the kindly grandfather figure who cared for her? The personality of the man in front of her was no longer as clear as she thought just a few minutes before. Her whole world became more complicated. Lizzie wasn't sure what would happen next.

The ladies stood watching as Jack tried to assess the old man while waiting for the ambulance to arrive. The flickering of the fire pit light started to fade until all they saw was the red flashing lights guiding the EMTs to Thomas.

"I just don't understand," Lizzie muttered to herself as she stood in the corner of the patio. Gertrude stood next to her in silence. "Gran, I just don't understand what Mr. Thomas did. Why would he do that to Eliza?"

Lizzie no longer felt like a confident adult. Once again she felt like a child searching for a solid place to stand with her grandmother.

"Pray, Lizzie. Just pray," Gertrude said.

The group stood in silence as the stretcher carried Thomas Abernathy out of the Clydell's backyard and toward the ambulance with Avery in tow. Lizzie watched as her husband raced to his truck to follow behind.

"Lizzie? Are you coming or not," said Jack as he climbed behind the wheel.

She stood in her backyard, glued to the ground, and looked toward the sky unsure of what to do next. A quiet whisper slipped from her lips as she shook her head.

"No."

CHAPTER TWENTY

After the ambulance left for the hospital, the conversation between the women flooded the room. Hurried voices went over and over details until Lizzie couldn't take any more. She struggled with what she heard and couldn't sit still.

"Quit your pacing, girl. You'll wear a hole into the carpet if you aren't careful," Blue shouted. "Plus, you're making me dizzy." She walked across the room to stand near the opened window.

"Gran, it was Mr. Thomas' father? His father!" Lizzie was still in disbelief. "Did you ever suspect that? Did you know his family? I just don't understand." Lizzie paced across the living room and next to the couch where Abi sat. Her friend reached up her hand and clasped it around Lizzie's wrist.

"Sweetheart, sit," said Abi.

Gertrude thought for a moment and then spoke. The stress of the evening had taken a toll on her, just not in the same way as Lizzie.

"To be honest, no, but it doesn't surprise me as much as you'd think. His daddy was a mean man. Cruel. I wasn't allowed anywhere near Greer Abernathy."

"I wonder if your dad suspected his involvement. There wasn't anything about him in the diary, was there?" asked Lizzie.

"No. There were sections near the end where my father alluded to possible suspects, but he didn't list any names. It was all just ramblings as he had aged."

Everyone in the room stood quiet and still. Jack had gone to the hospital to be with Avery so that he wasn't alone in a strange facility. As a sheriff's deputy he was usually able to get more information from the hospital staff, making him a helpful asset in an emergency.

"You have to remember one thing, Lizzie," Gertrude started.

"If you tell me that times were different one more time..." Lizzie muttered.

"Well, they were," interrupted Blue. "You can ignore it all you'd like, but it's the truth. Now, don't assume where your grandmother is going with this one. Take a seat and listen."

"If Greer had a hand in it, it wasn't like Thomas or even his brother had much choice. Back then we did as we were told. His father was heavy-handed. If Thomas had disobeyed him, he wouldn't have stood a chance. He was a little boy then. His daddy would have gotten physical most likely if he said anything, even with his older brother. There wasn't anyone to save us if parents like Greer Abernathy started swinging."

"You're taking that as an excuse for the way they treated your aunt? Did you read the same details that I did, Gran? The details may not be crude or crass, but it's clear. They raped her. Your aunt was raped. His family did that to her." Lizzie was inconsolable. She felt betrayed as her grandmother made excuses for the man who tore her family apart.

"What would you have me do, Lizzie? Hate him? This is Thomas Abernathy we're talking about. Do you not remember how he loved you and cared for you after your parents died? He's a mainstay at the church. Everyone loves him. Again, I remind you that he was a child when this happened. You can't blame a child."

"I can't believe you're defending him. If I'm held responsible for what I did, then he's held responsible, too." Lizzie flew up the back wooden staircase to her home's second floor in a rage, leaving the women in the kitchen. She slammed the heavy wooden door sending echoes throughout the quiet house.

"Oh, that temper," said Claud.

"It's just like when she was a teenager all over again," said Abi.

"Just let her go. She needs to cool off. We'll talk about it later," said Gertrude to her oldest and dearest friends.

"Do you think she'll come around?" asked Claud.

"I don't know. She's got such a problem with forgiveness. I just can't understand why she won't let go of the anger and just relax into grace."

"She can't because if she does that then she has no one else to blame for the death of her parents," said Blue. "She can't explain it if there isn't anyone to blame."

The friends sat in silence as they waited. Gertrude knew that Blue was right. It was exactly what Lizzie had been fighting all those years. Lizzie couldn't come to terms with the idea that sometimes bad things just happened.

***

Lizzie sat on the edge of her bed with her feet hanging down the side, her thoughts muddled and conflicted. She should be at the hospital awaiting news of Thomas Abernathy's health. He was a surrogate grandfather to her from the time she was a little girl. Now, he felt like a stranger.

She reached across the bed to her nightstand where the diary lay. If her grandfather suspected the Abernathy family she wanted to know his thoughts. She flipped through the pages with frantic panic until she found an entry written later in his life.

***

Diary of Alston James: 19 July 1968

"It is time to come out of the shadows, stop being afraid, and put evil away."

I'm not sure who said it, but it keeps sitting in my mind. It's time to come out of the shadows. I've lived there too long. I've kept Anne there with me. I've focused on forgetting. Each Sunday You remind me that I must forgive. The evil will continue to grow inside me if I don't forgive. My anger will never affect him, but it will rot me from the inside out.

Ephesians 4:31-32 says, "Let all bitterness and wrath and anger and clamor and slander be put away from you, along with all malice. Be kind to one another, tenderhearted, forgiving one another, as God in Christ forgave you." I haven't forgiven. The man who did this isn't with us any longer. He's facing his judgment from a far more fair and merciful judge than I would be. I can't keep blaming his son. He suffered as I have suffered. He carries the weight. It is up to me to forgive and lift his burden.

My Lord, please extend the grace that You have showed to me to the transgressors of Eliza's pain and suffering. It has gone on too long.

Alston closed the diary. He wanted his final entry to be one of forgiveness. "This should have ended years ago."

The anger and fear had lived under the surface of his life for decades. Old now, he was no longer able to carry that weight. His wife had passed years ago but his daughter had remained to be the bright shining spot in his life. Her son and daughter-in-law had recently married. His life was good, and he recognized that.

Walking into the church building, Alston saw Thomas Abernathy. He had prayed in the same pew at the same time every day for decades. Alston slipped into the second pew without interrupting his prayers. Alston glanced up at the stained glass window to the right of him. It was the story of the prodigal son. It was a story of forgiveness and acceptance. It was a story of grace.

Alston let his hand fall softly on the shoulder of the man in front of him before he spoke.

"Thomas, son, why do you come here each day to pray?" Alston asked.

With tears in his eyes, Thomas turned to look at the man behind him. He knew who it was at the sound of his voice. He grew up with the elderly man always in his eyesight and his thoughts.

"Sir, I pray for forgiveness for what I have done."

"And, what's that, son?"

"Sir, it's my fault that your family has suffered. This church is where I destroyed your sister. I'm so sorry." Resting his elbows on his knees, Thomas bent and leaned into his hands.

"I shouldn't have taken this long to reach out to you. Thomas, I forgive you. Do you hear? It has taken me far too long to acknowledge it. I thought that I was just struggling with my own fears and anger. In my old age, I've come to realize that you, too, have suffered. You have suffered by your father's hand and are a victim just like Eliza and Eldridge. I often suspected that you were involved, but I no longer hold you responsible. You were just a child. You didn't know what you were doing."

"But if I hadn't told my father, sir, your sister and her friend would have stayed living." Thomas became emotional and overwhelmed.

Alston moved to stand at the end of the pew next to the weeping man. Alston held out his hand. "Please, Thomas, you have to forgive yourself. God loves you, and so do I. It just took me a while to realize that I had to give you the same grace that I receive. You are hurting, and God wants to heal that hurt."

"I don't know if that's possible." Thomas took the elderly man's hand and cried.

***

Reaching for her Bible, Lizzie looked up the verse that her great-grandfather referenced in his diary.

"Great, you're preaching forgiveness, too. That must be where Gran gets it," Lizzie said into the air as she lay against the headboard of the bed. She had to get out of the house. Her legs needed to stretch, and she needed to rest somewhere where others weren't. The sun hadn't quite set, so she still had a little bit of time. She grabbed her purse and jacket, and then headed downstairs.

As she hit the last step on the staircase she saw that the gals had moved into the sitting room.

"Sweetie, are you going to the hospital?" Gertrude asked her granddaughter.

"I'm going to the park. I need to think. You're welcome to stay as long as you want. I just need to be alone. You can let yourself out."

Lizzie was out the back door with nothing more than a wave. She hopped into her Suburban and turned around in the side yard. Gertrude stood watching her through the open curtains as she drove away.

"I hope you find the peace you need," Gertrude prayed as she watched her granddaughter turn into a cloud of dust down the dirt road.

***

Lizzie stopped the vehicle in front of her favorite entrance to the park. She left the Suburban parked on the street rather than driving around to the side lot. Even though it wasn't a dangerous area, with the sun setting Lizzie felt safer with her vehicle close by in case she needed to leave. Unlike the other times she came here to pray, Lizzie felt determined and forceful, not soft and seeking.

As she walked toward her favorite park bench, Lizzie noticed a white rose that had dropped onto the walking path. It could have been left behind by a wedding procession as they made their way to the park for photos. Perhaps it was a lonely rose that hd broken from the bush when children played too close to the flower beds. She stooped to pick it up.

White for forgiveness, she thought.

Lizzie sat down on the bench underneath the large tree. She leaned back into the wooden slats and looked up at the stars. The church building across the street was open in the evenings for those who wanted to pray, but she needed to be in the open air where she could see the sky in all its glory. She felt like she could look through the stars tonight and speak directly to

God. Lizzie had been through Sunday School for enough years as a child to know that she could pray anywhere. For her, the combination of nature and family connections to the park made her feel safe when things were tough.

She sighed and began to think. Looking around to confirm that she was alone, she began talking out loud.

"Lord, I don't know what you are expecting me to do with this. I know that with You all things are possible. Yet, this feels like a load that I can no longer carry. I am so weary, Father. So angry. I feel as though it's been one trial after another. First it was my parents, and now I'm facing this situation with Mr. Thomas. I understand You want us to give forgiveness and grace, but in a situation where there is a murder it seems so wrong."

Pulling out her cell phone, Lizzie started searching her Bible app for the word *forgiveness*. Shocked, she saw page after page returned in the search results.

"Psalm 102:3: He forgives all your iniquities. He heals all your infirmities." Lizzie clicked on another search result. "Matthew 6:14-15: For if you forgive other people when they sin against you, your heavenly Father will also forgive you. But if you do not forgive others their sins, your Father will not forgive your sins."

Without warning, Lizzie burst into tears.

"You'll forget me? You'll stop forgiving me if I can't forgive the murder of two young teenagers? I need you Lord. You've taken so much from me. You took my parents and now you're taking Mr. Thomas. You'll take Yourself from me, too?"

Instead of anger, Lizzie felt true despair. She tapped the screen on her app to find another reference in scripture. She needed to find something that justified her anger toward Thomas. No matter what she read, Lizzie found the command to forgive others. Verse after verse confirmed to Lizzie that she had to ask for forgiveness to live out her faith in full.

She began to pray again and soon she found herself confessing her own sins as Thomas had confessed his. She cried out for forgiveness for her role in her parents' car accident. Lizzie had prayed for forgiveness in the past, but this time she felt an overwhelming peace as she said the words. She felt a peace that erased the guilt that had held her captive for the last twenty years.

Opening her eyes, she looked toward the church across the street. Her eyes landed on the stained glass window that her great-grandfather had always mentioned in his diary. In bright colors she saw The Parable of the Prodigal Son. Lizzie knew exactly what she had to do.

She had to accept the grace that the Lord had given her, and she had to extend the same grace to Thomas.

CHAPTER TWENTY-ONE

Lizzie walked through the hospital's front doors. She stood inside the large, glass rotunda that housed the welcome desk and admission cubicles. She looked around the space for signs pointing toward the Emergency wing when she spotted Jack near the elevator with his cell phone in his hand.

"I was just trying to call you," Jack said as he reached for his wife. He pulled her close by the sleeve of her shirt and gave her a tight hug that melted the stress away. "Are you okay? Your grandmother said that you left a few hours ago. I was getting worried since it was getting dark."

"I'm fine. I needed to be completely alone for a while before I could sort out what I needed to do."

"Did it work?" Jack looked at his wife before he led her to a bank of chairs against the wall of windows that overlooked the parking lot.

"It did. I think that I've finally figured it out. I know that I've been difficult to live with, Jack. I do. It's been all coming to a head as Gran says. I think I've finally made sense of it. Sitting alone in the park, I had my moment with God."

"Your moment?" Jack asked. He had the confused look on his face that Lizzie loved so much. It caused his nose to wrinkle and his laugh lines by his eyes to dance back and forth. It never ceased to amaze her how wrinkles looked good on this man.

"I learned about forgiveness, Jack. I need to give myself forgiveness and grace. Scripture was jumping out at me left and right tonight. I had to let it go, Jack. I can't move forward unless I realize that I can't hold onto all the heaviness of that night." Lizzie leaned back into the chair and tilted her head to look outside toward the stars that she loved so much.

"This is all about Mr. Thomas and what happened tonight?"

"No, in fact, it went beyond that. I finally forgave myself. I know that I didn't cause my parents' accident. I get it now."

Jack grabbed his wife in a hug that seemed to melt away any stress remaining between the couple.

"I knew you'd get there," he said with a smile. "What made the difference this time?"

"I understand now that the anger is just going to eat me up. Alston taught me that. He taught me that God will give us the grace and forgiveness we need to make peace with ourselves. To do that, we need to forgive others first. I can't keep going in circles, Jack. It's going to eat me up if I do."

"You have no idea how good that is to hear coming from you."

Lizzie held her husband's hand. "I can't explain it, but I feel lighter. I feel happier. Isn't that strange?"

"Not at all. It sounds like you've finally found peace. In finding what happened to Eliza, you found what you needed yourself."

Lizzie hadn't thought of it that way, but her husband was right. She thought that the journey through the diary was about finding out what happened to Eliza. She had never been so wrong.

"What do you want to do about Mr. Thomas?"

"I want to see him, Jack. I have to make sure he knows I forgive him before it's too late."

"Then, let's go." Jack took his wife by the hand and led her to the elevator that led to the cardiac unit. The short ride gave him just enough time to fill Lizzie in on the latest updates.

As soon as they stepped out of the elevator, Avery's stomach dropped.

"Avery, how's your grandfather?" Lizzie asked while she gave him a hug.

"The doctors think that they caught it in time. It was a heart attack, but it wasn't massive. They expect him to head home before the end of the week. I didn't expect to see you here. Are you all right?" Avery's face showed the effects of stress and worry.

"I'm not here to hold a grudge, Avery. I've made my peace with the situation. I hope that you can, too. We can't carry around the sins of our past, especially when what happened was out of our control. The choices your great-grandfather made that night were his and his alone. Your grandfather was just a child. Children can't hold onto the guilt of the bad things that happen in life. It's taken me a lifetime to figure that out."

Avery sat down in the nearest chair. He looked shocked, and like the weight of the world had been lifted from his shoulders.

"Lizzie, thank you. Do you think that you could tell Gramps that? He's so worried that he'll lose the special relationship that he has with you."

"That's why I came here. I need him to know that I understand."

"Let's go see him then. He's resting but awake," said Avery as he led her down the hall to Thomas' room.

Lizzie peeked around the corner and saw Thomas. To her, he looked like he had aged a decade in a few hours. His head was leaning back on a stack of several pillows. Eyes closed, his breathing was a little more labored than usual. Lizzie wasn't sure if it was his health or the stress of the situation, but she was glad that she came when she did. She eased herself onto the edge of his bed and took his hand into hers.

"Mr. Thomas?" she whispered.

"Lizzie. I'm so glad to see you. I wanted to apologize, honey. I am so sorry for what I did." The elderly man started crying softly as he turned his face away from her.

"Now, now, Mr. Thomas. Please don't cry. I understand. I do. You were a child. You didn't do anything wrong." Lizzie leaned over to give her old friend a hug. "I want you to know something. My Grandpa Alston forgave you, too. He never blamed you once for what happened. The sins of our fathers are not our own. We have God's grace, Mr. Thomas, and we have to share that grace with each other."

Thomas wiped his eyes with a handkerchief that Avery handed him. "Are you sure about your great-grandfather? He told me that he forgave me, but I was never really sure that he truly felt that way. He loved his sister so much. That's not something you can live through without harboring blame."

"No, sir. My great-grandfather didn't live that way. There was no grudge against you. It's time to forgive yourself like he forgave you." Lizzie reached into her bag for her great-grandfather's diary. "Here, I'll show you."

Lizzie spent the next few minutes going through the diary with Thomas and Avery. With each entry she could see the stress and fear roll off not only Thomas' face but off Avery's as well. As she read the final entry, Thomas reached for her hand.

"Thank you, sweetheart." He brought Lizzie's hand to his parched lips and gave her a kiss. "You've done this old man a load of good tonight. I've been carrying that burden for years. I have been scared of you finding out for so long."

"You don't have to be scared anymore, Gramps," said Avery.

Lizzie placed the diary back into her bag and returned to sit on the foot of the bed. "If you'd like to do something for me you can tell me about my Aunt Eliza. I don't mean the details of this ordeal. I want to focus on her life, not her death. Did you know her?"

"Lizzie, dear, I adored your aunt. She was a good few years older but she always took the time to spend a moment with me at church or as we were walking to school. She was a gentle soul." Thomas shifted to sit up higher in bed. "Everyone loved her."

"It sounds like they did. I would have liked to meet her."

"I wish you could have. It doesn't surprise me that she never recovered from what happened though. Her spirit was so loving that she didn't understand the pain and anger in the world. The world lost a brilliant light when she died."

Lizzie smiled at the picture that he painted of Eliza.

"Gramps, how did you avoid becoming involved in the activities of the Klan with your father?" Avery stood against the wall across the room with his arms crossed over his chest. "That must have been hard for you to deal with as a child."

"I was always a disappointment to my father. I wasn't able to handle the same types of things that my brother could. I wasn't able to slaughter the animals on the farm during killing times. I never was able to reconcile what they did to Eldridge and Eliza. I think he had given up on me."

"Lucky for you," said Jack. He had been so quiet that Lizzie had almost forgotten he was in the room.

"I don't know that my mother would have let him if he tried. I remember the night that he took me to watch what they were doing. She was screaming and begging him to leave me alone. She didn't stand a chance. My father was a rough man who didn't mind taking a hand to her any more than he did to me or my brother. I think my mother was beat worse that day than I was for running away."

"What do you mean?" Avery lowered himself into the chair next to his grandfather's bed. "I don't understand."

"I told you that I was behind the tree that night. It scared me beyond anything that I had ever seen. I wasn't expecting the screams. The look on their faces as the men hooted and hollered around them was a fear that I can't wipe from my mind. I ran. I waited for a time when my father wasn't looking, and I ran. I ran till I couldn't stop. I didn't have a neighbor to turn to or other family that wasn't involved so I didn't know where to go. My mother was damaged after the beating she took, so I couldn't expect her to protect me. I hid in the barn for the night. It took him until the next afternoon to find me. I thought I wasn't going to live after that beating."

Lizzie sat listening in disbelief. Her grandmother had told her of Greer's cruelness, but she didn't expect to hear that he unleashed it upon his own family.

"Mr. Thomas, I'm so sorry you had to go through that," said Lizzie.

"Gramps, your life had to be difficult. I never knew. Mama didn't talk about it much."

"I wouldn't expect that she would. She wanted to be out of reach from the world my father created. He was a cruel man."

"Gramps, you need to talk to her about this. She doesn't know much about this period in our family, and I think you could clear up a lot of her questions. She needs the chance to heal, too."

Thomas reached out a hand to pat his grandson on the shoulder and smiled. "You're a good boy. I think I'll enjoy having you here if you stay."

"Speaking of staying," said Lizzie, "I think we've overstayed our welcome. We need to let you get some rest so you can heal. We'll need you back at the church soon." Lizzie reached over to give Thomas a hug goodbye. Standing in the doorway to the hospital room, she noticed that she wasn't the only one that looked lighter.

"Walk us out?" Lizzie asked Avery.

"Sure thing. I'll be back, Gramps." Avery walked over to hold the door open for his new friends.

The threesome walked down the hall toward the elevators. "Do you feel like you'll move back to Everett Springs, Avery?" Lizzie asked.

"I'd say there's a good chance of it now," he responded with a wink.

Lizzie turned to Avery and gave him a hug. "Your grandfather is like family to me, so that means you're like family to me. Don't forget that. None of this need ever come up again. It will stay just between us. It will be our secret."

"I've been thinking about that." Avery leaned against the wall and put his hands in his pants pockets. "I might have an idea that you'll like."

EPILOGUE

Lizzie walked through the bright grass of the cemetery until she saw her family plot. No longer was the cemetery a place where Lizzie dreaded to go. She felt at home among the rows of headstones and flowers. Lizzie knelt down in front of her parents' grave, careful not to mess up her skirt. She ran her fingers over her parents' names as she read them in her heart.

"I miss you, but you'd be proud of me," she said with a smile. "You'd be happy about today I think."

After a quiet moment, she moved one plot over to her grandfather's marker. She dusted off the base of the stone. "Miss you, Pops. Gran does, too."

She moved again to the sit in front of headstone for her great-grandparents, Alston and Anne James. She needed a place to gather her thoughts before the day started, and it was fitting that she chose this spot. She glanced over her shoulder to see Jack standing next to her grandmother and the gals near the gates of the cemetery. She couldn't help but smile when she thought of how far they had come in the last six months.

"Thank you, Alston, for including your heart and your faith in your diary. It has been a key to healing for our family and for the Abernathys as well. I think you'd like where our families ended up. It took me a while, but I finally understand the lessons that you wanted to leave behind. No one is too far from God's grace and forgiveness, not even those who carry heavy burdens. You'd be proud of Thomas. He fought against his father's way of life and dedicated himself to taking care of your family and your church. He has given us love and respect for decades, and he did it in your precious sister's memory. We're learning about her life, Gramps, and it's great. Thanks for making sure we could find Eliza."

Lizzie kissed her hand and placed it on her great-grandfather's headstone. She knew that his spirit wasn't there to hear her, but she felt closer to him after their conversation.

Lizzie looked over at Eliza's headstone. She smoothed the front of her skirt before moving to stand next to the monument.

"Aunt Eliza, I am so thankful for your life. I'm so sorry that it had pain and sorrow. I pray that you are finally at peace. Your family will never forget you or Eldridge." She paused to look toward the section of graves where he would lay for eternity. "You'll both live on through the stories we're about to tell. They took your life, but they didn't stop your kind spirit. Your story will inspire us to respect and love each other. Your legacy is going to live on. I promise. We won't let hatred win."

Lizzie stood back to take in the full view of the cemetery before joining the others. A lot had changed over the last two seasons. She tilted her head back, closed her eyes, and let the bright summer sun land on her face. Warmth spread down over her into the places where stress used to live. Lizzie was finally relaxed and at peace.

People began to gather near the speaking tent. Lizzie smiled when she realized that the group included descendants from all three families. The children and grandchildren of Eldridge's siblings came from as far away as Oklahoma. Along with Gertrude and Lizzie, several cousins made the trip in Eliza's memory. Avery Abernathy's mother and father came to support Thomas as he took a public stand against the KKK's actions in the county. Other small groups gathered together in support of their own losses. Avery's idea to plan a family memorial for Eldridge and Eliza had turned into a full-scale community history event.

"You had a wonderful idea," Lizzie said as she stood near Avery.

"I couldn't have pulled it off without you." Avery leaned to bump his shoulder against Lizzie's.

As organizers of the event, Avery and Lizzie took a seat near the podium with the other speakers. Gertrude sat to Lizzie's left as she prepared for her presentation on the preservation of the cemetery. Other speakers sat waiting for their turn to share the history of the area during the 1930s through the Civil Rights Movement.

Lizzie was impressed with the way the speakers handled the horrifying details of the KKK's actions during the period. Each presentation was given in a way that was approachable for the audience without sugar coating the facts.

After the speakers finished, everyone walked up the hill for the unveiling of a new memorial. Dedicated to the lynching victims in the area, the twenty-five foot tall monument sat upon a base inscribed with the names of fourteen victims in addition to Eldridge. Genealogists in Gertrude's Tuesday Night Genealogy Gathering provided research that turned names and dry facts into lives the people of Everett Springs could remember.

Unlike the weeping angel that comforted Eliza in her time of need, this monument supported an angel of hope that reached toward heaven in joy and praise. It was Avery's idea to make the monument that celebrated life rather than mourned death. Lizzie couldn't have been more pleased.

Lizzie walked to the front of the group and waved her hand in the air to get their attention. Avery followed behind her and set up two wooden folding chairs, one for Gertrude and one for Thomas. As she gazed across the faces of her family and friends, Lizzie felt a hand sliding across her back. She looked up to see Jack smile at her as he stood by for support. She turned back to the group and took a deep breath to stop the shaking in her knees. Then she saw her family.

Blue gave her a wink and a thumbs up.

Abi blew her a kiss.

Claud patted her eyes with a handkerchief and whispered, "We love you."

Lizzie had everything that she had ever wanted. She had her family.

"Good morning, and thank you for coming. My name is Eliza Hines Clydell, but you can call me Lizzie. My friends and I have one last thing that we'd like to share with you before we start the picnic over at the church." Lizzie turned her head and smiled at her grandmother. "We would like to tell you a story about why we're here today. It all starts with a girl named Eliza and the people who loved her."

You can find more free short fiction and updates on upcoming works at **www.stephaniefishman.com**

Thank You

Thank you for reading *Finding Eliza!* I hope that you have enjoyed meeting Lizzie, The Gals, and the rest of the characters from Everett Springs.

Reviews are Important

If you loved this book, please take a moment to write a short review on the website where you purchased it. It will help others find the book and my work, and it would mean a great deal to me. Readers are why we write. It isn't for accolades but for connections. I would love to hear how you connected with the characters and story in *Finding Eliza*.

Are you a book nerd, too? Join me over on Goodreads (**www.goodreads.com**). You can join me, peek at the books that I'm currently reading, and leave a review of *Finding Eliza* for others as well. It's another way to help me share my words with the world.

Author's Note & Resources

I remember the first time I learned about lynchings in my history class. I was growing up in the Deep South, and as I looked at the faces of my classmates, it struck me that I could be sitting in the midst of a legacy of pain. I could be friends with the descendants of both aggressors and victims. As I fell in love with family history and began my journey in genealogy, I dug deeper into the pasts of my ancestors. Eventually, I found my first slaveholder in Virginia. I started thinking back to that moment in the classroom, and my earlier realization took on a deeper meaning: If I was related to a slaveholder I could be related to a member of a lynch mob. This part of history became real to me. It became something that I had to confront.

My family holds generations of people on both my maternal and paternal sides who wanted to fight for equality in their own ways. Whether it was a simple statement or an act of social justice, it surrounded me, and for that I am thankful. I will never forget several things that we were taught by my grandmother as her mother taught her.

Every person has a name.
Every life has value.
Every story needs remembered.

The story of Eldridge and Eliza is fiction, but it could just as easily have been true. The time line of laws that Lizzie discovers is real. Interracial marriages and relationships were illegal in some parts of the United States as recently as 1967.

I encourage you to learn more about this horrendous history so that we can prevent it from repeating in the future. We also have an obligation to remember those victimized in this fashion. Their stories must be remembered so that we can not only shine a light into the darkness but also to give a legacy to their deaths. Our country faces a great divide on many civil issues, and if we are not careful behavior like this could raise its ugly head once again when emotions and beliefs collide. Violence is never the answer.

For those wanting to learn more, here are some wonderful resources that I discovered during my research. Some websites contain descriptions or photos that may be upsetting to some. As a homeschool parent, I like to share what I learn with my daughters. This list of resources is intended to help educate not scar, so please use your judgment in sharing these websites with others.

The American Experience: The Murder of Emmett Till

The Murder of Emmett Till is a fascinating website to accompany the PBS special about the fourteen year old Emmett Till who was brutally murdered by a lynch mob in 1955 after whistling at a white woman.
http://www.pbs.org/wgbh/amex/till/

George H. White and Ida B. Wells Lynching Index

This website contains a wealth of information including books, videos, and even pop culture references. While it may not be the most beautiful or high-tech site, it is one of the most complete resources I have yet to find.
http://nathanielturner.com/lynchingindex.htm

Georgia Lynchings Project circa 1875-1930 (Emory University)

A team of researchers at Atlanta's Emory University took an analytical view of newspaper articles and reports of lynchings in the state. This site breaks down the commonalities, including the alleged crimes given in each murder. It is amazing to see the number that could be attributed to interracial relationships. Although most are listed as rape, I'm left to wonder how many could have been similar to *Finding Eliza.*
http://dev.emorydisc.org/galyn/

The New Georgia Encyclopedia: Lynching

Learn about the history of lynching in the state of Georgia, including frequency, location, and some of the most famous cases.
http://www.georgiaencyclopedia.org/articles/history-archaeology/lynching

The Mary Turner Project

In 1918, a "lynching rampage" took place in South Georgia leaving twelve dead, hundreds fearing for their lives, and even more evacuating the area to hope for safety. Mary Turner and her infant were among the victims. The goal of this project is to remember the victims who never received justice.
http://www.maryturner.org/

Pinterest

Other resources related to the subject matter in *Finding Eliza* as well as fun tidbits (and even lemon square recipes!) can be found on my *Finding Eliza* board.
http://www.pinterest.com/stephpfishman

About the Author

I chase dead people. I've grown up hearing family stories all of my life. In 1998, I picked up a new hobby as a way to pass the time with my grandmother. I now perform genealogical research for clients as well. I love to discover and share the stories of our ancestors. The words found in documents like marriage records and newspaper articles tell the stories of our families. In addition to providing research services, I enjoy creating narratives of family stories for my relatives as well as the relatives of clients. I am also active as a presenter speaking to genealogy groups and societies on topics related to family history research.

I've been a freelance writer for several years writing mostly on the subject of family history for blogs, websites, and genealogy societies and publications. I've also been a ghost-writer for areas ranging from air conditioning to the food service industry. I've enjoyed writing about family history much more than Chinese food.

I'm a 14-year veteran homeschool mom who tries her best to raise creative and curious kids. Two have survived into adulthood, so we can't be all that bad at it. The youngest is a triple threat: writer, musician, and artist. I'm hoping to work on a few projects with her in the future.

My favorite book will always be Rebecca by Daphne DuMaurier. I remember sitting in the classroom after school as my eighth grade English teacher introduced me to it. I had read everything on our list for that grade so she gave me her favorite titles to read instead. I also learned that at age thirteen I didn't enjoy Steinbeck but I loved Orwell.

During high school and college I bounced between creative and nonfiction writing with even a stint on a community college newspaper. I was just too nervous to tell anyone about it. Very few people read my words so it surprises me that my parents knew I wanted to be a writer before I was able to speak it aloud. As I got closer to a milestone year I decided to break out of my fear and start writing my books with the goal of sharing them with others. *Finding Eliza* is a fortieth birthday present to me. I hope you've enjoyed it.

I'm in love with the Oxford Comma. I'm hopelessly addicted to having my heart ripped out by BBC dramas. I love to insert references to history, pop culture, and humor into my writing and conversation. I currently have purple hair. I believe Joss Whedon can strike creative lightning at whim.

Official Biography

Stephanie Pitcher Fishman is an author and professional genealogist specializing in Midwestern and Southeastern United States family history. She is the author of seven family history research guides in the Legacy QuickGuide series on topics including religious records, census records, and state-specific research techniques. She has also written articles and blog posts for websites such as Archives.com and is a co-founder of The In-Depth Genealogist. She is also an active member of the Ohio Genealogical Society volunteering by lecturing on topics such as Plain Religions, Quaker research, and introducing family history to children. Her first novel, *Finding Eliza,* was published in 2014. To learn more, visit: **www.StephanieFishman.com.**

Connect with Stephanie

Email: **stephanie@stephaniefishman.com**
Facebook:
www.facebook.com/StephaniePitcherFishman
Facebook Group:
www.facebook.com/groups/SPFforReaders
Twitter: **@stephpfishman**
Pinterest: **www.pinterest.com/stephpfishman**

Acknowledgements

My thanks to…

My daughters, who are my world. Caitlin: I wouldn't have written Lizzie's first words during NaNoWriMo without you telling me that I could. Erica: You are my hero. I am so proud of you and the family you love so beautifully. Amy: I love you with all my heart.

My parents, all three of them. I'm blessed with three who love and support me, who fed me a steady diet of literature and story games, and who took me to bookstores just as often as playgrounds. They are truly the reason that this book was born. My mind builds characters and worlds because of the stories we created on living room floors and under covers before bedtime.

My family, especially my cousin Christian. Without their constant support (and endless Facebook and text messages of encouragement!) I would have stopped writing at the first stumble. Marc, my sisters, my uncle, my grandparents, my cousins… I am blessed beyond measure. I wish that Granny and Roy could see me now.

My friends, both those I claimed in childhood and those I met as an adult. You've all ended up in here. Whether it's your cemetery, your coffee cup, or your car, there are traces of you in all I do. A few of you even inspired The Gals.

A special heartfelt adoration to Dede Nesbitt and Andrea Johnson Beck. Without you ladies I'd be sitting in a puddle with no creative words, no book, and many, many fewer days of smiles. God brought me through it with the two of you. Your creative gifts inspire me, your characters entertain me, and your prayers sustain me. The wicked humor is a total bonus. Love you ladies.

My writing group, The Otters. You, ladies and gentlemen, have kept me sane. I look forward to the many adventures and oddly normal Google searches we will have together in the future. Thanks for holding my hand while we float. If you are writing, please find a group to call home.

My editor, Staci Troilo. I don't have enough thanks to show my gratitude. You gently and respectfully told me when I needed to move and change, and this book is better for it. You're my ace. Thank you for everything!

My beta readers, who refined me. You helped me give clarity and form to characters and ideas. Your feedback took a story that I loved and made it better.

Special thanks to my sister of the heart, Susan. I can't compress a lifetime into one sentence. All my love to you, your super hero, your beautiful little party planner, your mama, and a nod to heaven for your daddy.

Last, but most definitely not least, my God. I'm thankful that He had plans for me.

"For I know the plansI have for you," declares the Lord, "plans to prosperyou and not to harm you, plans to give you hope and a future. Jeremiah 29:11 (NIV)